DEAD AND DOGGONE

THE BEELER LARGE PRINT MYSTERY SERIES

Edited by Audrey A. Lesko

Also available in Large Print by Susan Conant

A New Leash on Death
Creature Discomforts

Dead and Doggone

SUSAN CONANT

BEELER LARGE PRINT
Hampton Falls, New Hampshire, 2003

Library of Congress Cataloging-in-Publication Data

Conant, Susan, 1946—
    Dead and doggone / Susan Conant
        p.   cm.
    ISBN 1-57490-466-3 (alk. paper)
1. Winter, Holly (Fictitious character)—Fiction. 2. Cambridge (Mass.)—Fiction. 3. Women journalists—Fiction. 4. Women dog owners—Fiction. 5. Alaskan Malamute—Fiction. 6. Dogs—Fiction. 7. Large type books. I. Title.

PS3553.O4857D43 2003
813'.54—dc21   2002154544

Published in Large Print by arrangement with
The Berkley Publishing Group,
a member of Penguin Putnam, Inc.

BEELER LARGE PRINT
is published by
Thomas T. Beeler, Publisher
Post Office Box 659
Hampton Falls, New Hampshire 03844

Typeset in 16 point Times New Roman type.
Printed on acid-free paper, sewn and bound by
Sheridan Books in Chelsea, Michigan.

For my mother,
Dorothy Morrison Conant,
and in memory of two pointers,
Jock's Great Stuff
and Jock's Little Nonsense,
my Stuffy and my Nonny,
with love from
the one-pup litter.

In acknowledging the generous help of the Committee for Responsible Research in Cambridge, Massachusetts, I must emphasize that the animal rights group in this book is not modeled on any real organization. All places and institutions in this book are fictional or used fictionally, and all characters are entirely imaginary.

Many thanks to Jan Dale, expert groomer, and to Joel Woolfson, D.V.M., for help with this book. Any errors in grooming and veterinary matters are mine alone. I am also grateful for the assistance of one of Dr. Woolfson's patients, my Alaskan malamute, Frostfield Arctic Natasha, C.D., my incarnate muse.

CHAPTER 1

MY NAME IS HOLLY WINTER. IT COULD BE WORSE. Buck and Marissa were counting on a boy. They had the name all picked out: Depth of Winter, to be called Dep. Any normal parents might have had second thoughts about sticking a kid with "of" for a middle name, but lots of Marissa's golden retrievers had it—Buddy, Susie, and Ren were all "of Winterland"—and the dogs had never objected, so I suppose my parents, or, as they always said, my sire and dam, didn't think a person would mind, either.

It's also possible that Marissa, who had a more advanced human social sense than Buck does, foresaw that the kids at school might laugh at somebody with the middle name "of." My own name isn't quite so embarrassing, but it's bad enough. I'm sure that Marissa didn't mean it to sound funny. She was a kind person. Even though I lost her eight years ago, I still miss her all the time. In his own way, Buck is gentle and sweet and even a bit shy, which is, I think, why he started breeding wolf hybrids when he got so lonely right after my mother died.

Or maybe the only reason I escaped a worse name is that I was the third litter in a row—nine goldens in the first, eight in the second—and my parents had used up their current stock of stellar names. Or maybe they were so amazed and disappointed at having produced only a human one-pup litter that they didn't bother thinking up a better name.

That's probably not true, though. In fact, Marissa used to claim that my father was so delighted with me

1

that he tried to register me with the American Kennel Club. I think she was joking, but it is true that as soon as Buck adjusted to the strange way I barked, he was proud of me. He has been ever since. I can tell. When I got my B.A. in journalism, he started addressing my mail to Holly Winter, U.D., which, in case you didn't know, is an advanced obedience title, Utility Dog, and Buck's idea of a compliment.

Even so, ever since I moved to Cambridge—and declined his offer to share the house in Maine with him and his wolf dogs—he's been a little hurt. When he feels hurt, he can act petty. For instance, he never admits to reading *Dog's Life*, but I know he subscribes, and I know he's still sore at me because after every issue comes out, he finds a way to correct some tiny error in my column. Admittedly, he knows more about dogs than I do. He knows more about dogs than any other person I've ever met, except my mother, but what he'll let me know he noticed is always trivial. In a column that came out a couple of months ago, I called a C.D., Companion Dog, a "degree." Not a week after that issue came out, Buck and I just happened to have a conversation in which he used the phrase "obedience title" thirty or forty times with a heavy emphasis on "title." You won't find the word "degree" in the American Kennel Club Obedience Regulations, but so what?

"That's precisely what you could have pointed out to your father," Rita told me. She's my second-floor tenant. She also called him a master of indirect communication. Cambridge psychotherapists talk like that. I've explained to her that Buck's indirect communication can't be so bad because I always understand what he means even though someone else

2

might not. Rita just nods and says, "That's what's wrong with it." Even though Rita is very good to her dachshund, Groucho, she can sometimes be an enigmatic know-it-all when it comes to people. And Buck isn't all that indirect. For instance, last Christmas, when he tied a red ribbon on one of his wolf dog pups and left it under the tree, where it chewed up five of its fellow presents, it just meant that he hated to think of his thirty-year-old daughter living alone in the city with only one dog. That's what I was more or less down to at the moment.

More or less? As I told Buck, if the average Alaskan malamute equaled five or ten other dogs in strength, IQ, and looks, Rowdy equaled at least two or three other malamutes. To me, I added, he was worth the endowment of my neighborhood school, a place called Harvard, and when it came to brains, he was better endowed than most of the faculty. So I needed a big dog? Mine weighed eighty-five pounds of muscle, I reminded my father. And beautiful? His coat shone silvery gray and white, and I liked his face, an open face, no dark marking on his muzzle and no black mask around his eyes, which, as I reminded Buck, were that very dark brown that's so desirable in malamutes. Do you know what a Siberian husky looks like? Enlarge him. If he has blue eyes, turn them brown. Shape them like almonds. Round the tips of his ears and set them wide apart on his head. Give him an even plumier white tail, an even pinker tongue, and an even bigger smile than he needs, and he'll look like Rowdy, not, incidentally, his real name, which I didn't pick. I didn't pick the name Rowdy, either, even though it suited him. By the time I got him, he responded to it, but that's another story.

This one started with a dog fight that broke out on Walden Street in front of Quigley Drugs, only a few blocks from my house, which is the red one at the corner of Appleton and Concord. I'd walked Rowdy past Quigley Drugs before, and the place had always worried me. It looked like a regular house, but you could tell it was a drugstore because over the front door hung a tilted sign positioned to crash on any customer who opened or closed the door. Since the sign had hung like that for years, I'd always assumed that no one had ever gone in or out.

Even before the day of the fight, I knew from the barks that erupted whenever I walked Rowdy by the store that there were dogs at Quigley Drugs, but I hadn't realized that they were in fact the magnificent pointers who showed up at dog training with their rather odd owners once every few months. I should have guessed. The Cambridge Dog Training Club meets at the armory on Concord Avenue, and I'd noticed that the pointers and their handlers walked home after class. The connection came to me as soon as I saw the woman standing in front of the store, on the cracked, weedy blacktop where you'd expect a front lawn to be.

The lights at the armory turn everyone a greenish purple, but spring sunlight didn't flatter her, either. She was a scrawny little thing somewhere between forty and seventy, cracked and weedy like the blacktop, with great folds of Shar Pei wrinkles dripping from the bones of her arms. When we got nearer to her, I could see that what looked like a mask was at least a quarter inch of suntan-colored foundation makeup. The fuchsia ringlets on her head must have been a wig. She wore an oversize pink baby dress and a pair of open-toed sling-back high heels that matched the dress and clashed with the hair.

4

A cork-tipped cigarette dangled from her lips, and coral lipstick filled the cracks around them.

"Come, Max!" she was screeching. "Come to Mama! Here, Max!"

If she'd shown up at dog training every week, she'd have learned to say his name first, then the command: Max, come. It didn't seem to matter to Rowdy, however; he was fascinated. When he dragged me to within a few yards of her and was about to introduce himself, across Walden Street bounded the errant Max, a lithe black and white pointer with a good head and a long, fluid stride.

Rowdy must have outweighed Max by thirty pounds, and my malamute's double coat of thick fur made him look even burlier than he was, but, in spite of his heft, he was no bully. Until the pointer tore into him, Rowdy probably assumed he was in for nothing more than some harmless rough-and-tumble or a ritual exchange of growls. As it was, the fight broke out, as some do, with none of the customary preliminaries, no long moments of raised hackles, no questioning snarls, none of the circling around that gives each dog time to assess the other's true intentions. One second, Max was streaking toward us. The next second, Rowdy had torn the leash from my hands, and the two dogs had hurled themselves into a snarling mass of slashing teeth and writhing fur. It sounded as vicious as it looked, an inhuman exchange of high-pitched yelps of pain, rumbling battle cries, and throaty canine obscenities.

Within seconds, Rowdy was on top, but Max's neck was twisting sharply around to position his teeth close to my big dog's soft, vulnerable throat. Rowdy had two moves open. If he kept Max pinned, he could dig his oversize canines into the back of Max's throat. But if, as

5

looked likely, Max managed to wriggle out from under, Rowdy could barrel into him, open those great malamute jaws, and crush the pointer's pretty muzzle.

The sudden, brawly shock of a dog fight, the primitive wailing, the guttural intimidations, the unpredictable lunges and slashes that can kill your dog or brand him a killer—all of it impels people to add human yells to the noisy chaos. We did. It takes a lot of self-discipline and more than a few old scars not to stomp into the fracas and try to snatch the first collar your hand meets. The lesson I've learned is that you always, always get bitten. If you have to grab, go for a tail, but be sure someone else goes for the other one at the same time. Better yet, run for a bucket of water or a streaming hose.

No more than twenty hour-long seconds after the fight started, I spotted the sprinkler irrigating the patchy lawn and scrubby privet in front of the triple-decker beyond the drugstore. I vaulted over the hedge, got a good grip on the sprinkler, cleared the hedge again, and brought the fight to a drenched end.

We made a ludicrous foursome there on the blacktop, two dogs indignantly shaking off water, two women gripping collars and ducking to avoid the spray. I tossed the sprinkler back over the hedge and checked Rowdy out. He'd always hated water, especially on his underbelly, and he'd taken plenty, but he'd shaken it off quickly and, with it, the disappointment of having had the most thrilling moments of the past year so quickly and liquidly interrupted. His big red-pink tongue was hanging out in a joyful, lopsided grin. His damp white tail was sailing merrily back and forth. He'd already forgiven me for spoiling the fun.

"I can't find any damage," I said. "How about you?"

6

She didn't answer me. She was too busy talking to Max, who was straining at his collar in eager anticipation of Round Two. "Mama is going to put you right back where you belong," she cooed. She dragged the protesting pointer past the beat-up green station wagon in the driveway and around the side of the store, then reappeared. Fat globules of makeup were rolling down her cheeks. I was afraid her whole face was going to dissolve and slide off, and I wasn't eager to look at whatever lay underneath.

"It takes a gutsy pointer to go after a malamute," I said. I meant it, but in the human negotiation ritual that follows a dog fight, I'd made a clumsy move. According to unwritten rules, each person expresses concern for the other person's dog. Eventually, if all goes well, the people then find some way to agree that both dogs are to blame, even though each person remains convinced that the other's dog started it.

" 'Go after'!" she yelled at me. "Max didn't start that."

Rowdy, of course, really hadn't started it. He'd never started a fight. He'd never backed down, either. He expected the same of me. I wasn't about to let him watch me knuckle under.

"Max obviously started it," I said. "The minute Max saw him, he could hardly wait to tear into him. You're lucky Max is still alive." That's true. When Alaskan malamutes fight, they go for a kill. That's why it's dangerous to train them as guard dogs. I didn't tell her that.

"If I find one scratch on Max," she screamed, "I'm suing you. That's a damned bloodthirsty wolf is what that is."

My bloodthirsty wolf was sitting at heel and, for

7

once, looking up to read my face.

"This is an obedience-trained Alaskan malamute." I spoke slowly and quietly. "Cambridge has a leash law, and he was on leash. Max was running loose."

It was below the belt. Any dog escapes once in a while. I'd never once seen Max running loose in the neighborhood. Even so, I tried to sound calm and self-confident, and I tried to defuse things. "Look, dogs will fight. I don't think Max is hurt. Let's check him out."

We did. One of these days, I'm going to be able to put Rowdy on a long down—that is, order him to lie and stay put—leave, and know that when I return, he won't have budged an inch. As it was, I downed him, tied his leash to a peeling drain pipe at one corner of Quigley Drugs, and followed the bizarre little woman through the gate of the rusty chain link fence into a backyard landscaped by dogs and lush with emerging city weeds.

A true dog lover is someone who never remembers your name and never forgets your dog's. At some time, I'd probably been told the name of the woman I assumed to be Mrs. Quigley, but the lovely pointer bitch who shared Max's yard was, I remembered, Lady. Like Max, she was white with black spots over the body and a few black patches on the back. Both pointers barked a little as they ran up to us. Pointers, I should say, are not mean-tempered. True, they won't cover a stranger with wet kisses the way malamutes will. But most pointers are sweet, friendly dogs with an aristocratic dignity that Lady lacked. Max had that regal bearing, but the little bitch was pathetically love hungry. While I made the kind of fuss over her that she deserved, the woman tried her damnedest to find something wrong with Max, but there wasn't a mark on him, thank God, not a bleeding ear, not a single puncture.

8

"Look, I'm really sorry this happened," I said. "I'm sure Max just didn't like another dog on his turf. He's gorgeous. They both are."

She lit a cigarette.

"Number three pointer in the Northeast last year," she said. At least she spoke my language. I assumed she meant Max, who had a winner's arrogance. "And entered on Sunday. A torn ear would've blown that."

"I'll watch for him." I smiled. "We'll be there."

"Sissy," she said, sticking one Dragon Lady claw toward me.

For a second, I thought she meant me, but I caught my mistake.

"Holly," I said as I took the claw. "I've seen you at dog training." I'm not one of those people who like to have canaries and parakeets perch on their hands. Sissy's fingers felt like fleshless bird feet. "I feel terrible about this. I love pointers. I've always admired your dogs."

That did it. Wet and cold, I had to stand there and listen to a catalog of Max's wins, an impressive list, then a discourse on Sissy's hopes for Lady, then a history of complaints about cow-hocked, pigeon-breasted pointers placed ahead of hers by fools of judges. I thought the adenoidal whine would never stop.

I finally managed to edge my way toward the gate. "I'm a little chilled," I said. "I think I'd better get home and dry off." I sneezed.

"Allergies?" She looked delighted.

"Just chilled, I think."

"Myself, I suffer something terrible from allergies. Pollen. Hay fever. Bees. Bees is my worst."

"Not dogs, I hope?" I asked jokingly.

"Dogs. Cats. Name it, and I'm allergic to it." She

9

sounded as proud of her allergies as she'd sounded of Max's wins. "My allergist says I'm a fool. Last time I see him, he goes, 'You're a martyr to your dogs. Get rid of them dogs, and you'll breathe a free woman.' 'Get rid of my dogs?' I go. 'Not on your life. My husband or my kid but not my dogs. Just give me a shot for it,' I go, 'because I've got a big show coming up, and no doctor's making me pull my Max.' "

My mother didn't believe in allergies. "Allergic to dogs?" Marissa would say. "Hah! Allergic to life." Buck, in contrast, doesn't doubt the existence of a true allergic response to dogs any more than he doubts the existence of evil itself. To Buck, dog allergies are simply the rhinolaryngeal stigmata branded on by the devil to mark his own. Sissy obviously didn't share his view.

"Well, good luck on Sunday," I said.

Just as I was about to open the gate, Max must have smelled or spotted a bird. If you've even once seen a beautiful dog on point, you know what Max did. Pointing is sudden and dramatic. Max's whole body tensed up, he lifted his right forepaw, he pointed his nose toward whatever he'd identified as game, and he froze in that posture. Other breeds—German shorthairs, setters, Vizslas, mixed breeds, lots of dogs—point, too. But one look at Max showed which breed had perfected it.

CHAPTER 2

FROM THE WAY MY FATHER BELLOWS INTO THE PHONE, you'd guess he looks like a moose. You'd be right. The point of his roaring was a request that I didn't need, at least not a mere two hours after Rowdy's fight with Max. He and Clyde were arriving in Cambridge on Saturday. Could I put them up?

Most of Buck's wolf hybrids are kennel dogs, but if you ask Buck, he'll swear that each one has a turn as house dog at least once every few weeks. By coincidence, every time I showed up in Owls Head, it just happened to be on Clyde's day in the house. A born gentleman, Clyde was unobtrusive, neat, undemanding, and, in short, the perfect houseguest. Even if he hadn't been, I would never have made Buck feel unwelcome, and not just because he insisted on giving me the down payment for this house when I couldn't find an apartment in Cambridge that would take dogs. I mean, Buck is my father. The bad news wasn't Buck himself, anyway, or Clyde, but the purpose of the visit, or rather, the consequences for me. It's fine if Buck wants to barnstorm for wolves at dog shows. I just don't want him around when I'm in the ring, and he was coming to town to do his wolf exhibit at Sunday's Masconomet Dog Show, for which I'd registered Rowdy about six weeks before. There went my fat registration fees.

After I hung up, I wished Rita were there so I could talk to her about it, but she was on vacation and wouldn't be home until a week from Saturday. The problem wasn't that Buck can be embarrassing to be seen with at a dog show where everybody knows he's your father. Of course, he can be embarrassing. He goes around buttonholing all the American Kennel Club delegates about getting the AKC to recognize wolf dogs, but I'm used to it, and everyone else is used to it. Everyone remembers my mother, and everyone except Buck realizes that it's just his lost cause.

The real problem is that he loves to watch me handle a dog in the ring, and he will not believe that he makes me nervous. He doesn't move. He doesn't make a sound. He doesn't have to. Naturally, since he doesn't do anything wrong, he can't understand why I don't want him there. My mother always showed her own dogs in breed and obedience. She was a better handler and a better dog trainer than I'll ever be. I'm not trying to compete. And Buck has never once made the comparison. Out loud. In fact, he just stands there towering over everyone else with his oversize features scrunched up in the kind of stupid grin that parents reserve for the accomplishments of their offspring. In the previous three or four years, I'd managed never to register a dog for a show Buck was going to attend, and when I registered Rowdy for Masconomet, I'd had no idea Buck would be there.

Rita was away. I called Faith Barlow. Faith breeds and handles malamutes. I'd hired her to handle Rowdy in breed, the type of competition that's sometimes called conformation. The winners are supposed to be the dogs that conform best to the official breed standard. I love obedience, but I hate showing in breed. It's the most viciously competitive sport in America. I hate it, and that's why I'd hired Faith. But I was worried about obedience, not conformation. No way was I going to handle Rowdy in the ring under Buck's watchful gaze. I told Faith just that.

12

"What the hell is wrong with you? You're acting like a jerk." Faith does not have the makings of a good therapist. "You're pulling a dog because Daddy's going to be there? What is this crap? How old are you?"

"It's just a policy I have," I said. "And please don't mention it to him."

"I won't have to. He'll read it in the catalog."

She was right. Rowdy's name and mine would be right there, under "Novice B Obedience."

"He won't necessarily buy a catalog," I said. Hah. "Besides, I'm not sure Rowdy's ready."

Her only response was the silence I deserved.

"Faith, I'm just pulling him out of one show. What's the big deal?"

Faith is tough. She gave me a long argument about how gorgeous Rowdy was and how I owed it to him, to her, to his breeder, and to myself to show him. She pinned me the way Rowdy had pinned Max. But no one turned a sprinkler on her. What she said next may sound innocuous, but anyone in the world of purebred dogs will recognize it as the ultimate weapon. Faith is half malamute. I told you they went for a kill.

"You owe it to the breed," she said.

She won, of course.

CHAPTER 3

IN MY FAMILY, THE DOG WAS THE SACRED ANIMAL, like the cow in India. Remember, God spelled backward is dog. Thus, my affair with my vet, Steve Delaney, should have felt like the seduction of a high priest. Maybe it did.

If you met him, you wouldn't blame me for having succumbed to temptation. Maybe it's sexist or old-fashioned, but I like tall men, and I don't find weak men attractive. Anyway, you could tell to look at Steve that he could heft Great Danes and Irish wolfhounds onto the exam table without straining himself. His eyes got to me, too. I liked that sleepy look that came from getting up in the middle of the night to answer the phone when a panicked owner called him. And I also liked his curly brown hair and the color of his eyes, deeper than Siberian-husky blue except when those baggy surgery greens picked up the flecks in the irises.

If Steve hadn't been a terrific vet, Dr. Draper wouldn't have sold him the practice when he retired. His only problem taking over from Dr. Draper was that lots of the female human clients started inflicting psychosomatic ailments on their pets to have an excuse to see him. Persian cats with headaches. Brussels griffon bitches with menstrual cramps. I ask you.

With this background in mind, you may find it hard to understand how I could have forgotten about Saturday night, but I had. The reason wasn't the occasion. Not everyone thinks of the annual dinner of the Massachusetts Society of Veterinarians as a big date, but, of course, I did. The dress was one reason I forgot.

"So what'd you find?" Steve's low, gentle voice rumbled over the phone.

I don't like shopping for clothes except from the L.L. Bean catalog, and L.L. Bean dresses are mostly shirtwaists made, I think, of the same plaid as the cedar dog-bed covers. Of course, the shops in Harvard Square have dresses that don't coordinate with dog linens, but Rowdy'd been with me every time I'd been in the square lately. The shops don't allow dogs, and I didn't trust him alone there, even tied up. People steal dogs, and he'd have gone with anyone.

"Oh, still trying to decide," I said. It wasn't easy to decide how to tell Steve that Buck would have to come with us. "I've got four days left. And guess what? My father's going to be here. He's bringing Clyde. They're doing an exhibit at Masconomet on Sunday."

"I, uh, hadn't planned on going. And I've seen the exhibit. Remember?"

Did I remember? At the Museum of Science, Buck and Clyde had been a big hit with everyone, including Steve. The trouble had begun afterward at my place. With no intention of provoking an argument, Steve had remarked that for the average person, a golden retriever makes a better pet than a wolf dog hybrid. Did I ever remember.

"Yes," I said. "You liked the exhibit. You said that Buck was well informed. And he doesn't have any hard feelings. He likes you." Buck doesn't hold grudges.

"Good," Steve said flatly. He wasn't giving me a lot of help.

"I can't just exclude him," I said. "I mean, he *is* my father."

"I know," Steve said. "You've mentioned that before

15

from time to time."

"He'll have a lot in common with everybody. He knows a lot about dogs. He won't embarrass you. If they serve oysters, he'll use the right fork. He knows not to drink out of finger bowls. He'll know to leave Clyde home."

"Did I say Clyde couldn't come? Bring Clyde. Bring your cousin Janice's twelve fox terriers I vaccinated free."

"Really, Steve. I know Janice wasn't very gracious, but she appreciated it a lot. I promise he'll behave."

"No," he said. People who train dogs have a special way of uttering that word when they really mean it. They don't shout it. They don't drag it out. They don't hesitate, and they don't make it sound like a question. They just say it.

"How could I explain it to him?" I asked. "He just would not understand."

"He'll have to try."

"No," I said. I train dogs, too, of course.

By the time I hung up, I was glad I hadn't wasted money on a new dress. That was when the moving van pulled into my driveway. Something else I'd forgotten.

My house is a barn-red wood-frame triple-decker. The first floor, which I occupy, hasn't been renovated yet, just spiffed up, but I gutted the other two apartments and did them over when I bought the building. Rita has had my second-floor apartment for ages, but the third floor had been vacant for the past month, ever since Alison Moss and her two cats moved out. I was sorry to see the three of them go. Alison was reliable. The rent from the apartments pays the mortgage, so I can't afford tenants who don't pay, and I can't afford vacancies. Especially if you consider that I

16

allow pets, my rents aren't unreasonable, but all Cambridge rents are high. "Ah, but it's worth it," people say. "Harvard is just around the corner." In my case, if you count the new Observatory Hill town houses, it's right across the street.

I'd met David Shane when he was standing, leash in hand, on the sidewalk eyeing the new buildings. I was walking Rowdy home. The dogs introduced each other. (Lonely? A flashy dog beats a singles bar any day and smells better, too.) Shane said what a beautiful malamute I had. Most people call him a husky or a husky-shepherd cross, but Shane knew right away. I said what a beautiful Irish setter Shane had. He said her name was Windy. I said it suited her. It did. The breeze was rippling her long red fur. I'm partial to Irish setters, anyway, but she was a beauty, good bones, an ideal head, and a lively air, maybe a little high-strung, but with no sign of real nervousness. Shane said he was an assistant professor and I told him about my job at *Dog's Life*. He said he'd look for my byline in the next issue.

That's how he ended up as my third-floor tenant. His looks and finesse had nothing to do with it, and neither did the fight with Steve. After all, I had met Shane and offered him the apartment two weeks before he moved in—that is, two weeks before that phone conversation with Steve—but the fight probably is what made me comb my hair when I heard the moving van.

Whether Rowdy heard the van, smelled a new dog moving in, or thought I was taking him for a walk I don't know, but he was bouncing up and down by the back door with such irresistible enthusiasm that I snapped on his leash—about a dozen hang on the hooks by the door—and took him with me. The van was a professional one. I was surprised to see it. Most people

17

here move themselves with U-Hauls. A Mercedes of dyed-to-match Irish-setter burgundy pulled up on Appleton next to the driveway. Shane and Windy got out.

"Welcome," I called. Snappy, huh? No wonder he fell for me.

"Holly Winter!" he said. "And Rowdy the Wonder Dog." You could hear the capitals in his voice. Some guys really know how to sweet-talk a girl.

The man was not stupid. Or ugly. And although he was not much more than thirty, he had none of Steve's sleepy boyishness. There was nothing rumpled about him. He was thinner than Steve, who'd always seemed to me more lean than thin, but he didn't look weak. Brown eyes and blond hair are an appealing combination. Even so, he wasn't really handsome, I thought. His face was better than that, asymmetric, angular, with high cheekbones. He was wearing one of those expensive leather aviator jackets over a white turtleneck that I think was cashmere. I didn't run up and touch it to find out. Rowdy was at least as delighted to see Windy as I was to see Shane, even though, when I'd asked Shane, he'd said she'd been spayed. Rita's old dachshund, Groucho, isn't altered, and neither, of course, is Rowdy—if he were, I couldn't show him in breed—so, I just can't have an unspayed bitch in the house.

Anyway, attraction between dogs is sometimes just friendship, and that's what Rowdy seemed to be making noise about. Once every three or four months, he'd bark like a normal dog. Ruff. Bow-wow. I'd also heard him yip, growl, snarl, whine, and howl. Most of the time, though, he talked the way he was talking to and about Windy: "Woo-woo, ah woo, woooooo."

I was used to it. If we'd been alone, I'd have answered back. Since Shane knew enough to know Rowdy was a malamute, he must have heard it before, too, but he laughed, anyway, and so did the moving men who'd opened the rear door of the van and were lugging out a seven-foot white leather couch. No claw marks showed on it. The leather hadn't been chewed, and the white was all white with no red hairs. It takes a brave man to have an Irish setter and a white leather couch.

The Mercedes. The couch. David Shane looked more than good for his rent, and it was hard to say which was more a purebred, I thought, Shane or his Irish setter.

CHAPTER 4

"JUST WHAT DID YOU THINK YOU WERE DOING? DID you think I wouldn't know who did this?" I shoved the handful of banana peels in front of Rowdy's nose, where he couldn't avoid smelling them. "There's no one here but you and me, buddy. Was I supposed to think I ate the bananas myself and threw the peels under the table?"

It was Wednesday morning, and I'd run him twice around Fresh Pond, exactly twice the distance I enjoy running, and while I was in the shower afterward, he stole the bananas from the kitchen counter, devoured them, then slunk off to play innocent. I found him curled up on the floor by the bay window in my bedroom, where the window seat is going to be someday.

"I know who did this," I added, shaking the peels again. Banana peels are slimy, anyway, and these were covered with dog drool, too. "You are a very bad boy."

He had the serious expression of the falsely accused, and without even bothering to lift up his big head, he raised his eyes and looked right at me as if to ask what I could possibly be going on about, but he also flattened his ears down. He knew what "bad boy" means. He'd heard it before.

"Don't you ever do this again," I said emphatically. "You be a good boy!"

He knew those words, too, and I knew he knew them. I rubbed the top of his head. After you speak your mind to a dog, it's important to let him know you forgive him. Besides, it was half my fault. I should have put the bananas away.

At ten, Faith Barlow picked Rowdy up and took him to a handling run-through. I spent the rest of the day finishing a column for *Dog's Life*, then tried working on a story, but it didn't go well. I'd been trying to do something with no dogs, just people, but every time I thought I had it, a Pekinese would spring up in someone's lap or a stray Lab would meander across a lawn.

With no dogs and no story, either, I quit at four and went outside to scrape paint on the north side of the house. It's just about impossible to get these old wooden houses to hold a paint job. You have to think of painting, like dog training, as a process, not a task to start and finish. It was one of those warm, humid days we sometimes get in the spring, which is to say, one of the four or five days a year when the temperature in Cambridge isn't above eighty-five or below thirty. I spent two mindless hours developing lead poisoning and thinking about loss. I reached a couple of conclusions. First, if you have to lose someone, better a good vet than a good dog. Second, if you have to lose a parent, better not to think about which one it should have been. Then a bee landed on my right hand and delivered one of those feeble early season stings. My week.

After Faith returned Rowdy and dashed off, I fed us both—not the same thing—and told him to take good care of the house till I got back. I had a meeting of the Cambridge Dog Training Club to attend. I knew exactly the kind of ferocious guard dog Rowdy was—none at all—but I didn't want him to suspect that I had less than complete confidence in him.

Until one of our members, Frank Stanton, died and bequeathed us the house at the good end of Appleton

Street—not that my end is bad—we took turns holding board meetings at our houses. At first, we were all so impressed by our new acquisition, our little English cottage nestled in the splendor of the neighboring Victorian mansions, that we tried to hold formal meetings. We didn't wear kennel clothes. We got nothing done. Before long we reverted to lounging around in jeans without worrying about mozzarella on the carpet and rings on the mahogany table.

Thanks to an unsuccessful attempt to scrape all the paint out from under my nails, I was the last to arrive. The others were already sitting around the table in the dining room. At first, we tried to call it the boardroom, but no one could say "boardroom" with a straight face, even though the room doesn't disgrace the name. It has white paneling, a fireplace with brass candlesticks on the mantel, and a genuine painting by Sir Edwin Landseer of one of his favorite subjects: a black and white Newfoundland. Ray and Lynne Metcalf, who have Clumber spaniels, were there, as well as Arlene, who has greyhounds. Ron Coughlin, the club treasurer, was at the head of the table, and Diane D'Amato was next to him, with Curly, her miniature poodle, in her lap. Try that with a malamute. You may have seen Curly. He's the little black dog who dances around on his hind legs and yaps out a song in the Snappy Bits commercial. Curly wasn't the only dog there, just the only canine board member. Hussan, Vince Dragone's Rottweiler, was on a long down in the front hall—Vince is our head trainer—and one of Barbara Doyle's shepherds, Freda, was behaving herself on the floor at Barbara's feet. The people were all talking and the dogs were all silent. I was glad I'd left Rowdy home. He'd have woo-wooed his way into the conversation.

22

After I took a seat across from Ray and Lynne, Ray turned to the woman seated next to him, the one person there I didn't know. "Mimi," he said, "I'd like you to meet Holly Winter. Holly, Mimi Nichols." He sounded uncomfortable about using her first name.

I wished I'd brushed the dog hair off my shirt and emptied my pockets of dried liver treats before leaving home. We shook hands. Hers had paint on, rather than under, the nails.

"Holly," she said. "I'm delighted to meet you."

She made it sound genuine. With the smooth, dark hair sweeping away from that oddly unlined, immobile face, she looked as if she'd have a wispy Jackie Kennedy voice, but hers was strong—not loud, just powerful. You could tell she'd be able to say "boardroom" without smirking. To attend the meeting of a dog training club, she'd put on a cream-colored dress made of something I couldn't identify. Silk and vicuna? Is that possible? The very rich actually *are* different from you and me. They wear mysterious clothing. What was she doing there? As I tried to think of something normal to say, I realized everyone else was having the same problem. I thought about asking her whether I could borrow the dress to wear to a veterinarians' dinner, but then I remembered I'd been disinvited.

"So, Holly, what have you been up to?" Ron asked.

Mimi Nichols's presence hadn't intimidated him too much. Ron moves with ease through all social worlds. Pipes burst impartially on the rich and poor alike, and anyone with any sense, regardless of income, defers to a good plumber.

"Not a lot," I said. Scintillating. "Rowdy got in a fight with a pointer. I have writer's block. I got stung by

23

a bee. Actually, it was my own fault. I knew there was a hive. Otherwise, it's been a great week. You?"

The look on his ruddy, round face let me know I'd said something wrong, but I couldn't figure out what. I didn't have time to try. Barbara opened the meeting.

"We have a lot to take care of, so let's get started," she said in that soft, fluffy voice that matches her soft, fluffy blond hair, but not her character. "First, I'd like to welcome Mimi Nichols. As you probably know, Mimi lives a couple of houses away, and she's interested in the petition. Mimi can only stay for a few minutes, so we'll start with zoning. Mimi?"

We were about to petition the Cambridge zoning board for permission to open the house as a library, or, really, to open it officially. A lot of people had used the library for years. The collection of books was and is incredible: stud books, breed books, books on training, handling, and gait, the breed quarterlies, histories, every book you'd ever want to read. All we were trying to do was let people in, but for zoning permission, we needed neighborhood approval. Typical Cambridge politics.

"As I understand the situation," Mimi said, "neighborhood concern centers on two issues, traffic and parking. Since you don't propose training or kenneling dogs here, dogs are not the real issue. As I've explained to Barbara and Ron, I may be able to suggest a solution to the parking." She gestured graciously toward them and gave us all the best smile she could manage without being able to move the muscles around her eyes. Fifty looking forty? Sixty trying for thirty-five? A lovely lady of uncertain age, certain surgery. "The principal use of the library, I believe, would be limited to daytime hours. Ten to five? Monday through Saturday. No Sunday use. Is that right?"

We all nodded yes. Once again, she did her best to smile. Nothing crinkled. I felt sorry for her. Maybe if she got a dog, she'd laugh enough to put some expression back. A Rhodesian Ridgeback, an Afghan hound, a Saluki, something as sleek as she was.

"As you're aware, St. Luke's has ample parking around the corner."

Faces fell. The church had given us a flat no. Twice.

"The problem is availability. After some preliminary checking, I believe that might work itself out. If so, traffic will be a nonissue."

She didn't say it, but the traffic—there wouldn't even be much—could enter and leave the St. Luke's lot from Brattle Street, which is busy, anyway. None of the people on Appleton would see or hear it.

"Yeah, but they've turned us down twice," Arlene said.

Ron looked hard at her and tapped his lips quickly with a finger to hush her. She got the message.

Mimi continued. "I'm also here to request your support in regard to another matter. As you probably know, in less than two months, the city council will be asked to enact a law regulating animal research in Cambridge. Of course, that includes research on dogs." She paused. If there's one thing dog lovers don't want to think about, that's it. She gave us a few seconds to ponder it, anyway. "St. Luke's has a strong commitment to social action. Right now, they're especially interested in the ethical treatment of animals. That is, you share what I assume must be a common concern."

I expected her to go on, but a big guy in jeans who looked as if he'd bulked up with free weights stuck his head through the door to the front hall. Mimi Nichols looked first at her watch, then, tilting her head to one

25

side, at Ron, who dutifully popped up, thanked her, and, of all things, helped her into no ordinary American trench coat. She had the manner of someone who had never put on a coat unassisted.

"We promised Mimi we'd only keep her a few minutes," Barbara said. "She has another meeting."

Like Ron, Barbara thanked her. Everyone else thanked her. I, for one, had no idea why. I expected to be told as soon as she left, but people just kept looking at each other. And at me.

"What's going on?" I asked. "Did I miss something?"

There were some uncomfortable laughs before we started to act like ourselves again. Ron went into the kitchen and came back with some cans of Bud and Coke. Money has its down side, I guess. You never know how people act when a rich person isn't around. That Mimi could afford unidentifiable clothes didn't necessarily mean she wouldn't have liked a beer, too, or at least a Coke. Anyway, with Mimi gone, everyone spilled everything except the drinks. I hadn't been all that stupid. I'd just been the only person to arrive after Mimi Nichols, so I'd missed the background.

"How was Holly to know that Edward Nichols died of a bee sting?" Lynne said kindly, but everyone laughed again.

"Stings," Barbara corrected her. "He got stung and went into shock."

"Oh, God," Ron said to me. "When you said it was your fault that you got stung . . ."

"It wasn't exactly Nichols's fault," Barbara said. "It wasn't the same. Apparently, he was supposed to carry one of those kits, but he forgot it, and he didn't get to the hospital in time."

"Obviously, I had no idea," I said. "She was awfully

26

nice about it. Who is she, anyway? What's the deal? I mean, everyone's been acting as if Princess Di had dropped in."

"The deal is that she's decided to take us up," Lynne said.

"The deal is that she's saved our sweet ass." Ron cleared his throat. "Sorry."

"She does causes," Diane said. "The latest is animal rights, and she's into grass roots. Cambridge animal rights. We're the grass roots."

"*You* may be," said Arlene, pulling her chair away from the table. "Speak for yourself. I don't know what those people are so worked up about. They just don't have anything better to do. I mean, it isn't as if Cambridge had any of those labs you read about. You know. Maybe there are some mice and rats, but so what?"

"Hold it," Ron said. "Holly still doesn't get who she is."

"Yes, I do. A woman who needs a dog."

"As a matter of fact," Ron said, "she already has three."

"Oh," I said. "What kind?"

"Pointers," three people said at once.

"Pointers, huh? I like pointers," I said. "Did I say something bad about them? All I said was that Rowdy had a fight with one. For all I know, she thinks Rowdy's a pointer, too."

"If you had a pointer, she'd know you," Barbara said coolly. "You'd know her."

"She doesn't show in obedience, does she?" I said. Hardly anyone shows pointers in obedience. Or malamutes, of course.

"No," Barbara said. "And she doesn't handle them

27

herself, anyway. Remember Libby Knowles? You know her, don't you?"

"She used to train all those goldens with us," Arlene said.

"I know her," I said. "She's good."

"You know, those dogs weren't hers," Arlene said indignantly. "They all belonged to other people. She does it for money."

"A hooker!" Ron said jubilantly.

"I know Libby," I said. "I hang out with her at shows sometimes. She's a good trainer. She's a good handler."

"And Macho Man takes care of the dogs," Barbara said.

"I thought he was a bodyguard." Lynne looked disappointed.

"Chauffeur," said Ron. "You know he lives there? He's the security man. He does everything. He's not a bad guy. He's real good with dogs, and he does some kind of dog rescue thing. Picks up strays. Stuff like that."

"Is she aware of that?" Arlene asked. "She didn't strike me as the rescue type."

"Of course. It's like the research law," Ron said. "Along the same line. Well, not exactly the same line, but, you know, it's all grass roots."

"If I have to hear any more about grass roots," Arlene said, "I'm going to turn green and need mowing."

"Look, let's cut it short," Ray said.

Ron laughed.

"Oh," Ray said. "No pun intended. Anyway, the story is that she worked things out with St. Luke's. Needless to say, she's a parishioner. That's one reason they're suddenly so enthusiastic about animal rights. She gives to them. She gives to that committee on animal research. She just doesn't take much credit. She's a very modest person. Anyhow, it's done. It's wrapped up. St. Luke's really only needs that big lot on Sundays. We pay a fee. We support the animal research law."

"Don't we already?" I asked. "I do."

"Actively," Lynne said.

"Can we give money? I don't think that's in the will," I said.

When Frank Stanton died, he left more than his house to the Cambridge Dog Training Club. Most people don't know precisely how much because my editor at *Dog's Life* thinks it's vulgar to discuss money, and she cut that part out of the article I wrote about his murder. I still haven't completely recovered from the shock of his death—and my unexpected involvement in the murder investigation. The one benefit of that whole mess, of course, was that it brought Rowdy and me together.

"As individuals we can donate money," Ray said. "The club can't."

Most of our members don't have any more to give than I do. A few do. The Metcalfs. Ron. A couple of others.

"Mimi Nichols is, in fact, a philanthropist," Ray said. "It sounds funny, but it's true. These people really do exist, and she's one of them. We're the community, and our part is community support. We give signatures. We write letters. We have handouts ready for the meetings. We put something in the newsletter. We talk to people. When the same kind of thing comes up again, we do it again."

"We should've been doing it all along, if you ask me," Barbara said. "This is not a joke. Nobody wants to think about it, but it's really serious."

Contact lens solution, deodorant, makeup, household

cleansers, herbicides, insecticides, almost all of them are tested on animals. In the name of science and medicine, dogs are crammed into tiny cages to wait their turns for vivisection. Of course, they're still dogs, so they try to protest. They try to call for help, but no one hears them. I'm not getting poetic. No one hears them because science and medicine remove their vocal cords. It's known as surgical debarking.

"If you want my opinion," Arlene said, "the whole thing is too political. And it's a straw man. I've seen the awful pictures, too, but those labs aren't in Massachusetts. They're in New Jersey. California. Here, it's just politics."

"This is Cambridge," Diane said. "Everything's politics."

"Exactly," Arlene said. "It's all just politics, and it's only mice and rats, anyway. Not dogs."

"That's not what I meant," Diane objected. Curly was still perched on her lap, turning his head back and forth, eyes bright. "What I meant is, sure, everything in Cambridge is politics. But I, for one, don't know anything about research labs. For all I know, the ones here do use dogs. How would I know?"

Dog people talk all the time. We talk at classes. We call each other up. Most of what we do at dog shows is sit around and talk. We talk about dogs, of course, and we talk about each other, but we don't talk politics, except the politics of the breed clubs and the American Kennel Club—not real politics. What dog people share is an interest in dogs. Otherwise, we're everyone: old, young, men, women, liberal, conservative. I knew that Vince was active in the Republican Party and that he might not be happy with the idea that we were forcing him into some left-wing cause. He didn't say a thing.

No one else wanted to talk real politics any more than Vince did. Instead, we argued about dogs, and it was pretty amazing. There we were, crazy about dogs, spending every Thursday night and some part of every day training dogs. Most of us subscribed to at least two magazines about dogs. I wrote for one. Some of us showed our dogs. Some of us bred them. Dogs were our life. And not one of us knew whether Arlene was right. Nothing but mice and rats? If she was wrong, I thought, it didn't matter what kind of hypocrites we were, left wing or right.

CHAPTER 5

A BIG DOG SHOW IS THE GENUINE GREATEST SHOW ON earth, a circus with all-day, nonstop action in twelve, fifteen, twenty rings, more hype and hoopla than Barnum & Bailey, more excitement than high wire with no net, and two thousand tame performing animals from every part of the globe—Tibetan spaniels, Chinese Shar Pei, Japanese chin, Finnish spitz, Australian cattle dogs, Rhodesian Ridgebacks, French bulldogs, Norwegian elkhounds, Belgian Tervuren, in every size from giant to toy, Irish wolfhounds, Great Pyrenees, and St. Bernards to papillons, pugs, and Pekinese. Almost anything in the world you really need, you can find at the concession stands: collars and leads in a rainbow of colors, rake combs, flea combs, mat combs, bristle brushes, slicker brushes, pin brushes, hound gloves, flea powder, ear powder, grooming spray, grooming shears, St. Aubrey Coatasheen, Ax-A-Dent stain remover, Wonder Fluff shampoo, Bitter Apple, Lust Buster (Cools Off Heat), free samples of Bil Jac, Eukanuba, Nutro MAX, Old Mother Hubbard, Science Diet, Martin Techni-Cal, and Natural Life. In case you're looking for nostalgia, you'll find the same hamburgers, pizza, and tuna sandwiches your high school cafeteria used to serve. Just as the song says, the coffee's good for cuts and bruises, and tastes like iodine. When you go to a dog show, never forget your own lunch. And don't forget your own folding chair. Your head will swim and you'll need to sit down. A big dog show runs on a tight, ordered schedule, but it still feels like the most chaotic show on earth.

The Masconomet show's big top was the Bayside

Exposition Center, just off the Southeast Expressway. In November, there's always a four-show cluster there, and, in the spring, Masconomet is the last indoor show of the season. When I pulled the Bronco into the parking lot at eight-thirty, mist was still rising from the harbor, but the show had already been open to the public for half an hour and open to exhibitors since six A.M. The parking lot held the usual collection of Winnebagos and other big RVs and vans with plates from New York, New Jersey, Virginia, Vermont, everywhere on the east coast and a few from far away—Ohio, Minnesota. To dog show people, distance means nothing. Some of the RVs had been parked there all night, and some had been driven all night. People leave work at five on Friday, drive all night to a Saturday show, spend all day there, then drive all Saturday night to make a Sunday show, drive home, and go to work Monday morning. They drive in comfort. You see few compacts, and you never have to wonder what's inside those RVs, vans, and big American station wagons. The white Winnebago in front of me had a bumper sticker on its rear that said "Caution: Show Dogs," and all around and above the caution, bumper stickers with pictures of Dobermans and Dobie-chauvinist proclamations—"Love Is a Doberman Pinscher," "Happiness Is a Dobie," "I Love Dobermans," and, simply, "Doberman Pinschers."

I was, for once, dogless. Faith had insisted on keeping Rowdy from Friday on to get him ready. Despite his objections, I'd always kept him clean, but I won't fuss over grooming the way she does. If I'm going to spend two hours working with a dog, I can always find something better to brush up than his coat. I'd gone to Faith's on Saturday to do one last training session.

Masconomet, I should add, was not Rowdy's first obedience trial. At the first one, he lay down at the end of the long sit, an automatic disqualification. At the second one, his long sit was perfect, and he stood up at the end of the long down—in other words, about five seconds before he would have got the first leg of his C.D., his first obedience title, Companion Dog.

Nobody expects anything of malamutes in obedience, but Vinnie, my last golden, got her C.D. with an average score of 196 (highest is 200) in three straight shows and went on to earn her C.D.X. and her U.D., and she wasn't my first Utility Dog, either, just my best. My dogs are carefully trained for obedience. They don't break on sits and downs. But Rowdy'd done it at two trials, and almost everyone I knew had been watching. I wanted that leg at Masconomet.

I showed my admission ticket at the door and got my hand stamped with purple ink. I expected to find Faith in the main handlers' area near the entrance, but I had to make my way through the crates, the grooming tables, the hair dryers, the handlers, and the hundreds of dogs into the main hall where the rings are, past the cafeteria, and down to the grooming area at the far end before I spotted her.

Under a loose white grooming smock, Faith was dolled up in a soft, fuzzy pale gray sweater and darker gray tweed skirt. A matching tweed suit jacket in a dry cleaner's plastic bag hung from one of the stacked-up crates nearby. For as long as I'd known her, Faith had looked in her forties. Her hair was blond going white and cut to require little grooming, but curly and soft around her face. She wore pearl stud earrings and had on pink lipstick and a trace of blue liner to highlight her eyes. In addition to handling Rowdy for me, she was handling someone's Siberian bitch that day, and she'd dressed to match the two silvery gray and white dogs. She looked super.

The Siberian was in her crate, and Faith had Rowdy on a grooming table, where she was using a vegetable brush to rub French chalk white into his feet to clean them for the show. In front and in back of Faith and Rowdy, to their left and right, were dozens of other handlers, dogs, grooming tables, tack boxes, and crates of all kinds—metal mesh cages, fiberglass crates, airline-approved polypropylene crates, Vari-Kennels, Kennel Cabs—lined up in rows and stacked on top of each other like a children's village of giant blocks. The white on Rowdy's coat was, as the ads say, whiter than white, and Faith's practiced hand had fluffed up his coat so it stood out everywhere and shone as if it would glow in the dark.

"Jesus," I said. "How'd you do that?"

"Professional secret." When she smiled, the dimples in her cheeks appeared.

Rowdy was evidently delighted with himself, thrilled with Faith's attention, and pleased to see me, too. From the top of the grooming table, he gazed around like a potentate surveying his nation. I made a fuss over him, and His Highness condescended to give my face a wet lick.

"He's looking great," I said to Faith. "You've done enough. I need him for a run-through. I've got to warm him up."

"Give me ten minutes. He's also got to be exercised." That's a little euphemism among dog people. She didn't mean a five-mile run.

"Sure. I need to check in, anyway, and I'd better say hello to my father." He'd arrived the day before, as

35

planned, but we'd taken separate cars to the show because he wanted to be there at seven to set up his exhibit. Also, Rowdy would be riding home with me. Although he and Clyde got along well, Rowdy lacked the emotional maturity to share a car with another dog, or that's what Rita said. "Oh, no," I said suddenly, glancing over Faith's shoulder. "Did you see her when you set up here?"

"Who?"

"Sissy Quigley. Down on your left."

"She must've just got here." Faith was using a metal comb to touch up the fur on Rowdy's forelegs, which the breed judge would carefully check for heavy-boned strength. "Loudmouth gossip. I wish someone would shut her up. You should hear the awful things she says about me. Anyway, ignore her. She's vicious, but she doesn't actually bite."

"It's just that I'd rather Rowdy doesn't see Max. They aren't exactly good friends. They got into something the other day, you know. Anyway, she looks weird, but she doesn't seem all that bad. I should probably say hello to her later."

"She'll give you an earful about me if she knows I'm handling Rowdy. And keep an eye on that good lead."

"Why?"

"Didn't you know?" Faith had begun pulling a wire slicker brush through the long fur of Rowdy's tail. "She won't take your wallet or your purse, but she'll take a good show lead, brushes, stuff like that. Everyone knows she does it."

"I didn't know. She trains with us sometimes, and no one's ever said anything. Everyone leaves stuff around. Are you sure? Doesn't she get caught?"

"She's sneaky about it. She's careful."

36

"I'll watch out," I said. "Anyway, the important thing is, I'd really like Rowdy not to catch sight of Max, if you can manage it. I don't want him all worked up. I'm nervous enough already."

"Take a deep breath, blow it out, and relax. What is this, anyway? Your eight-hundredth show?"

"No," I said. "I don't know. I'm not normally this way. How would you like to go and distract Buck while I'm in the ring?"

"Sorry," she said. "I've got Lilly, too." She waved the brush at the Siberian's crate.

"Don't worry about it," I said. "I'm going to check in. When do you need Rowdy for breed?"

"Eleven. Ring Two."

"No problem. We'll be done long before that."

I passed Sissy's part of the grooming area on my way to the obedience rings. Max was on top of a crate, and she was brushing him, a cigarette dangling out her mouth, red curls and tufts springing from her head. As the loudspeakers kept blaring out, smoking was forbidden in the grooming areas and everywhere else except the cafeteria. According to American Kennel Club regulations, it's also forbidden to exhibit dogs that have been "changed in appearance by artificial means." Unfortunately, the rule doesn't apply to handlers. Sissy was as garishly made up as she'd been last time I saw her.

By then, it must have been somewhere around nine, because that's when judging starts. Linda McNally was one of the Novice B stewards, and she wished me luck when I checked in.

"Why are you so nervous?" she asked. "You look green."

"My father's here," I said as I fastened on my

37

armband. "I hate showing when he's around. I know it's nuts, but he makes me nervous."

"Relax," she said. "Remember, it's only a dog show."

Only the Last Judgment.

I said hello to a lot of other people—obedience people are my people—and I started to feel a little better, proud that Rowdy looked so snazzy, glad to be a part of things even with my father watching. On the way back to find Faith and Rowdy, I noticed something I hadn't taken in before, that Sissy had set up with a lot of other pointer people. Partly as a carryover from the wonderful old benched shows, where all the dogs of each breed are benched together, partly just because they know each other, some people still tend to set up near other people showing the same breed. But Sissy and Mimi? I made my way toward them, through the narrow aisles between the crates and the grooming tables. I wanted to say hello to Mimi, and it seemed like a good idea to wish Sissy well, especially while Rowdy was out of sight. I make my living in the world of dogs, and I don't need enemies.

Although it was only the second time I'd met Mimi Nichols, I understood even then that she moved through life preceded, accompanied, and followed by retainers. The brawny young guy who'd escorted her from the meeting stood right next to her, arms folded across his chest, face impassive, as if literally to retain her, prop her up in case she fell. She wore a beige suit of something I thought might be raw silk or maybe something called shantung. It reminded me of grass cloth. Even in the harsh lights of Bayside, no wrinkles, lines, or expression showed on her face, but her voice was animated. She was talking to Libby Knowles, who looked, as always, young—twenty-five?—strong, healthy, and, if you admire Rottweilers, handsome. She had the muscular, compact, vigorous body of the breed, straight black hair, darkly tanned skin, a solid face, and a Rottie's eager, energetic expression. As usual, I resisted the urge to march up to her and say, "Hey, Libby, has anyone ever told you you look just like a Rottweiler?"

Instead, I marched up to Mimi, who held a show lead at the end of which pranced a pointer that would give Max more than a little competition, a sleek, shiny dog with a dark brown head, a large brown patch on each shoulder, and a mostly white body with the small brown spots called ticks. The correct way to describe his color is "liver and white ticked," but that sounds ugly, and he was far from ugly—stunning, in fact.

"Unbelievable dog," I said. With no tension on his lead, he held his head high and proud. Practically every American Kennel Club breed standard says that the ideal specimen looks intelligent, alert, and noble. This dog really did.

"Thank you," Mimi said warmly. "Holly Winter. From Cambridge Dog Training." You see? Not a real dog person. She remembered my name, and if she'd met Rowdy, she'd have forgotten his.

Libby, a true dog person, said, "Hi, there. That's Sunshine." She nodded toward the pointer and smiled. His pride was contagious. "Where's Rowdy?"

Like Faith, Libby was dressed up and even had on thin plastic gloves to protect her manicure. I was spiffed up, too, in a professionally starched white shirt, a black cotton sweater with no dog-nail snags, a denim skirt, and brand-new white Reeboks to match Rowdy's French chalk white paws.

"He's with Faith Barlow," I said. "She's handling

him in breed. I've got him in Novice B myself."

"Good luck," Libby said to me, then stopped rearranging the brushes, scissors, sprays, and miscellaneous grooming paraphernalia in her tack box, turned to Mimi, and added, "Novice B is for people who've already gotten a C.D. with a dog before. Holly used to have goldens."

The implication, not lost on me, was that if I'd always had malamutes, I'd have spent my life not qualifying in Novice A.

"Is that the second one?" Mimi asked me.

"Second?"

"C.D.—the second title in obedience?"

"No, it's the first," I said. "C.D. is the first obedience title. There are three classes, or really, levels—Novice, Open, and Utility. And there's a title at each level: C.D., then C.D.X, then U.D." As it was in the beginning, is now, and ever shall be. "There's also Obedience Trial Champion, of course." World without end, amen.

"Companion Dog," Libby explained to Mimi. "Companion Dog Excellent. Utility Dog."

When ordinary rich people like doctors and lawyers decide to take up show dogs, they read everything and pretend to know what they're talking about. Not Mimi. She didn't pretend to know anything, and she wasn't embarrassed about Libby's public tutoring.

"How many legs have you got?" Libby asked me.

A few more questions like that, and Mimi's face would've regained some flexibility.

"None," I said. "Yet."

"I don't know why you're bothering, with a malamute."

"I'm trying to think of it as a challenge." For Mimi's benefit, I added, "A leg means you've qualified at one

40

show. You need three legs for a C.D. And the others, too. You have to qualify at three shows under three different judges. We're trying for our first leg today."

Sissy heard me and moved in. She wore a flouncy, ruffled turquoise dress in a material I had no trouble identifying as polyester. Miniature enamel pointers were clipped to both of her ears. Another enamel pointer hung from a chain around her neck.

"I thought you were trying to show in breed," she said loudly. Ignorant snob. Trying, indeed. What she meant was that obedience is for dogs not good enough to show in breed, that it's a second-class sport for second-rate dogs. You hear that stupid myth all the time.

"Faith Barlow is handling him in breed," I said.

Two men moved in to flank Sissy. One was a hapless-looking young guy, the other, her companion from dog training. His age was as unguessable as hers, but where she was glaringly colorful, made up like a badly embalmed corpse, he was an entirely dark nonentity. If she looked like the deceased, he looked like the undertaker. When I'd seen them together at class, I'd never been able to decide whether he was her husband or her son. The hapless one, I now saw, must be her son. The nonentity, I assumed, was the husband—the pharmacist, Mr. Quigley.

I suspect that Mimi sensed some tension and, lady that she was, decided to smooth the social waters by introducing everyone to everyone else.

"I'm Mimi Nichols," she said, extending her hand to the older man.

"Austin Quigley," he said. "My son, Pete."

"I already know her, Dad," Pete said ungraciously. "I did a room for her. At her house."

"Baby, shut up," Sissy told him.

41

Although it's probably not what Sissy meant, Pete Quigley did have a baby face, and when he glared at his mother, he looked like a resentful infant about to hurl a rattle at her.

Mimi ignored the interchange. "Yes, of course," she said. "I think you know Libby Knowles. And this is Reggie Cox," she added, stepping aside and evidently expecting the bodyguard to move in and say, "How do you do?"

All he did was nod his head in acknowledgment. To my surprise, Sissy moved a step forward, and I had the impression that she was about to say something, but over her shoulder I caught sight of Faith gesturing to me.

"Sorry, I've got to run," I said. "Faith wants me. I said I'd exercise Rowdy." Mimi probably thought I'd picked a strange time to take him for a run.

As usual, my fastidious Rowdy refused to use the designated exercise pens, which he had always considered dirty and public. After I broke the show rules by taking him out to the weeds by the harbor, I returned him to his crate and then went to look for my father. I heard his voice even before I saw his booth.

"All dogs are descended from wolves," he was explaining forcefully.

Even from a distance—and I kept my distance—the exhibit looked good: large posters of white arctic wolves, a video display of some kind, and, of course, Clyde, wandering around at the end of a lead behind Buck, like a long, tall, rangy version of Rowdy, with big ears and wary eyes.

Sissy stood in front of the exhibit, bony arms akimbo, shrieking at Buck, almost spitting. "You've got no business bringing that thing in here. For your information, I want you to know that there are valuable show dogs here today."

I stayed long enough to see Buck draw in a gigantic breath, throw his shoulders back in that Teddy Roosevelt bull moose way he has, and start to bellow. Then I walked away. I'd wanted him distracted while I was in the ring, but not like that. I should have gone up to Sissy, loyally introduced Buck as my father, explained that Sissy had two beautiful pointers and that Buck used to have goldens, and got them talking to each other. Instead, I walked away.

It was a mistake to get Rowdy out of his crate when I was feeling so lousy. I did, anyway. Then I heeled him to the Novice B ring, where we waited our turn while I sweated. People who know will tell you that if you're nervous or upset in the ring, you smell like a stranger to your dog and he won't obey you. Those people are right. When our turn in the ring finally came, Rowdy's heeling on leash was bad. Just bad, not disqualifying. I don't think I made any handler errors. But I could feel myself sweating, and I could sense that stranger phenomenon. To Rowdy, I wasn't Holly anymore. I was some other person who smelled of guilt, shame, and disloyalty. After the figure eight, the last part of heeling on leash, I stacked Rowdy up for the stand-for-examination exercise, unsnapped the leash, and handed it to Linda McNally, who smiled at me and tilted her head a little to the side. Rowdy did fine. Next came heeling off leash.

"Are you ready?" Mr. Salisbury asked.

"Ready," I said.

That's a ritual. I was, of course, lying.

"Forward," he said.

"Rowdy, heel," I squeaked.

43

Rowdy was more or less with me, less rather than more, but if the dog stays within six feet of the handler, the judge is supposed to award a qualifying score for the exercise. The recall did us in. With Rowdy sitting at one end of the ring, I walked to the opposite end, turned, and, on Mr. Salisbury's signal, called, "Rowdy, come!"

Rowdy didn't. Instead, he shook himself all over, threw me a grin, and started to tear around the ring in circles. The crowd loved it. First, he just got laughter, then applause. The judge and the stewards loved it. I tried to catch Rowdy, and if he'd been on leash, I'd probably have succeeded. As it was, he got a running start, sailed out of the ring, steamrollered his way through a bunch of people, and leapt into the next ring, where Dorothy Barton was judging pointers. Pointer dogs. Max. I was in that ring only seconds after Rowdy. Bless Dorothy Barton. She swept in, caught Rowdy's collar, and brought him to a swift halt. If Max had gone for him? If someone had tried to break it up and been bitten? If he'd accidentally bitten a judge? I don't want to think about it.

Pretending that Rowdy was someone else's dog—and that my own was a golden retriever—I took him by the collar and led him back to the Novice B ring. I didn't say a word to him. Mr. Salisbury, who is really a lovely person and a good judge, asked me whether I wanted to complete the remaining exercises, the group sit and down. I didn't. A mean judge would have insisted.

With Rowdy back on leash, I led him to his crate and shut him in. The Siberian was in hers, and Faith was nowhere in sight. I sat on the floor and felt rotten. I felt guilty about my disloyalty to Buck and even more awful about Rowdy's misbehavior. I could almost hear my mother's voice asking me what she always asked when

44

a dog I'd trained acted up: "And just who taught him to do that? Just who trained him?"

But you want to know what obedience people are like? Ten or twelve people came up and told me worse stories about their own dogs. I heard about dogs retrieving dumbbells from other rings, leaping out of the ring to steal food from the spectators, relieving themselves in the ring, and trying to bite judges— sometimes successfully. Not one person tried to make me feel bad. As I began to calm down, I remembered what a good time Rowdy had had flying around in circles and playing the clown for everyone. These things happen. It's only a dog show.

But Sissy must have known how near a miss we'd had with Rowdy and Max. I'd been cowardly enough for one day. With Rowdy still locked in his crate, I wandered down through the grooming area to offer Sissy the apology she deserved. Rowdy hadn't started the first fight. Even if he'd run up to Max in the ring, he wouldn't necessarily have started another one. But he might have, or Max might have, and Rowdy certainly had disrupted the judging. For that, I owed Sissy an apology.

Before I saw her, I heard Max. He was howling in a way pointers usually don't, pitifully, frantically. He was in a big Vari-Kennel on the floor, and he was scratching at the metal mesh door, trying to get out. That's not normal. A show dog's crate is his home away from home, his den, his haven in the chaos of the show.

"What's wrong, boy?" I asked him as I walked toward the crate. "No Best of Breed today?"

I almost stepped on her.

The red clown wig was loose, starting to slip off, and scanty red fuzz of another shade was curling out underneath it. Her grotesquely made-up face finally had the best reason of all to look as if it belonged on a corpse. I must have lost my mind for a couple of seconds. For a brief instant, I thought Sissy had had an accident. Then I came to. There was no way she could have done it herself. She could not have taken that pair of big grooming shears and plunged them through the silly turquoise party dress into her bony chest. She couldn't have fallen on them and rolled over. She couldn't have done it, not by accident, not on purpose. Someone had made Faith Barlow's wish come true. Someone had shut Sissy up for good.

CHAPTER 6

"MY BEST GROOMING SHEARS!" LIBBY SAID indignantly. "Those happen to be Geib shears. Katana, they're called. You probably recognized them." I must have looked blank, but she went on. "You know what they cost me? Two hundred and ninety dollars. Mail-order discount. New England Serum."

"I've been using UPCO lately," I said. "United Pharmaceutical. There's no fifty-dollar minimum, and they carry most of the same stuff."

"Not these," Libby said.

"Two hundred and ninety dollars is a lot of money," I said.

"Oh, but they're worth it."

What kinds of human beings are these, you might ask, chatting about the cost of grooming equipment within hours of a murder? These are dog people. In shock.

One question popped into my mind—if a murder occurs at an American Kennel Club show, do the rules still apply? If so, Libby and I were breaking one of Masconomet's—namely, no chairs in the grooming areas. I'd unfolded mine, L.L. Bean, white, with a convenient carry strap, at the far end of the grooming area near the vacated obedience rings, and Libby had appropriated the judge's wooden chair from the Novice A ring. Maybe Libby's more of a professional than I am, or maybe looking like a Rottweiler decreases the need to have a dog with you all the time. In any case, she'd left Mimi's pointers in their crates, but Rowdy was with me, making up to Libby, muzzling her hands, swishing his white tail, and giving her one of those big-

47

brown-eyes looks meant to convince her that he thought she was someone special. Since he thought everyone was special, it was probably true. According to the American Kennel Club breed standard, the Alaskan malamute is not a one-man dog. According to my standards, this Alaskan malamute was an indiscriminate anyone-and-everyone dog, hopelessly flattering, maddeningly sincere.

"This is really a very sweet dog," said his latest victim. "Too bad he NQ'd."

NQ'd. Gave a nonqualifying performance. Washed out.

"It wouldn't have counted, anyway," I said. "Would it?"

"Of course it would."

"How could it? I'm sure they'll just scratch everything. What else can they do?"

"Oh, no. Sunshine took BOB." Best of Breed. "They can't."

When the judging of all the breeds is over, the winner for each breed enters the best in group competition for his group—sporting dogs, working dogs, terriers, or whatever. For Libby and Sunshine, the show was just beginning.

"I haven't heard anything official," I said, "but I'll bet this is one show that won't go on."

"I don't believe it."

"Libby, really. I mean, the woman is dead. She was murdered. You can't just go on holding a dog show around her body."

"Maybe you're right," she said. "The dogs are mostly too upset, anyway."

"I've never heard a pointer wail like that before. You know what I thought? I thought, bloodcurdling. There was that blood, and that unearthly wailing, and you know the way a really high soprano voice can shatter glass? I had this awful image in my head of blood curdling." My hands were starting to shake. I grabbed Rowdy's collar and pulled him away from Libby.

"It's just an expression. Blood doesn't curdle."

"I guess not," I said. "It doesn't curdle. It clots."

"Hey, pull yourself together. Getting morbid isn't going to do any good. It was just your bad luck that you found her. It doesn't have anything to do with you."

"It had something to do with someone. I feel terrible—I used to laugh at her. Not to her face."

"Of course you did," Libby said. "So did everyone else. She was ridiculous."

"She was pathetic. The baby dresses. The makeup."

"Nobody made her do that. Did you actually know her?"

"I used to see her at dog training. But I just really met her the other day. Rowdy got into a fight with one of her dogs."

"Max?"

"Yeah. But it worked out all right. Neither of them got hurt. Then I saw her today." I dropped my voice. "Faith told me that Sissy stole things."

"Everyone knows that."

"I didn't."

"That's because you don't show in breed anymore."

"I never did very much."

"If you had, you wouldn't feel so sorry for her," Libby said. "Being a thief wasn't the worst thing about her."

"So she was boring. And silly. I mean, it's so sad, Libby. For one thing, there was that pathetic need to look young. And for another, I practically didn't know

49

her, and she started telling me all about all these ailments, all her allergies."

"That was bull," Libby said. "She was a class A hypochondriac."

"I guess."

"All she wanted was attention. And that wasn't the worst thing, anyway. There was lots more. She said terrible things about people, and most of it was outright lies. Boy, was she ever jealous of Mimi. And she was jealous of me, too. And another thing is, did you ever hear her with that poor kid of hers, Pete? She dragged him to every show to haul her stuff in and out, and she treated him like garbage. I'm telling you, she was a nasty person. Look, there are vicious dogs, right? There are. We all know it. And there are vicious people."

"Libby," a deep voice said, "Mimi wants you." Reggie, his name was, the brawn.

"Thanks," she said. "I'll be right there."

"Someone's always right there, huh?" I said.

"It's not really like that. She's all right. She doesn't know anything, but I like her. Are you okay?"

"Sure," I said.

Okay means, of course, that my dog is with me and he's fine. Rita has a book called *I'm OK, You're OK*. That's how I am, except the other way around. The dog's okay, I'm okay. According to Rita, the hand that rocks the cradle really does rule the world. Buck and Marissa had a wooden cradle for me when I was baby, but I don't remember it, and you can't rock a whelping box, which is what I do remember, lots of whelping boxes filled with golden retriever puppies. When puppies are not okay, they whine and squeal so piercingly that no one else in hearing distance is okay, either. Okay is quiet puppies, soft fur, the sweet scent of

50

dog, and a correct canine-human ratio, eight or ten to one. With my quiet, furry Rowdy at my side and two thousand dogs nearby, I'd have been perfectly okay. Except for remembering Max.

Lieutenant Mickey De Franco had a bizarre resemblance to Santa Claus, the same curly white hair, the same round, red-cheeked face, the twinkling eyes, and an abdominal bowl full of jelly that would have earned him higher marks at the North Pole than at a police physical.

"You're from Cambridge . . . Concord Avenue." he read from his notes. "Ho."

I swear, if I'd spirit-gummed on the white whiskers and popped him into the red suit, he'd have asked me what I wanted for Christmas. What he did ask was whether I knew his cousin, Kevin Dennehy.

"Kevin's my next-door neighbor," I said. Kevin's a cop, too, but in Cambridge, not Boston. "My kitchen's his local bar and grill."

Kevin lives with his mother. Ever since Mrs. Dennehy abandoned the Catholic church for Seventh-Day Adventism, she won't allow alcohol, meat, or caffeine in her house. The Dennehy house is definitely hers, not Kevin's. A corner of my refrigerator is definitely Kevin's, not mine.

"So you're the dog nut," De Franco said.

"So to speak."

"Ho-ho." As Kevin told me later, his cousin was not born ho-hoing but acquired the habit while playing Santa for the Ancient Order of Hibernians every Christmas. Kevin says that no one else in the family even notices it now that they've made De Franco quit laying his finger aside of his nose, but maybe Kevin

51

made that up.

Rowdy was pulling on his leash and whining at the sight and smell of an array of American cheese slices, bologna, and olive loaf on a long table at the far end of the room. We were at one of the white-shrouded round tables, with the napkins and silverware shoved out of the way. The police had requisitioned the meeting rooms where dog show officials were supposed to be eating their free lunches. De Franco had drawn the stewards' lunch room. Judges get roast beef or lobster rolls, not cold cuts.

He picked up a fork and started tapping it on the edge of the table.

"They call your father the wolf man, I heard," he said. Tap. Tap.

As any properly socialized resident of Cambridge would have realized instantly, the man was obviously in therapy for the Santa bit. Every time he felt the impulse to ho-ho, he was supposed to tap-tap instead.

"He raises wolf dog hybrids," I said matter-of-factly. "And he does educational programs about wolves. He used to have golden retrievers," I added. There's no more ordinary, normal, respectable breed of dog than the golden retriever, except possibly the English setter.

"And you've got one?" He pointed the fork at Rowdy. "That's one of the wolves?"

"No," I said. "This is an Alaskan malamute."

It was a natural mistake. The hybridizers' ideal is a friendly, loving, trainable animal that looks like a wolf. In other words, if you want my opinion, wolf dog hybridizing is a silly and unsuccessful effort to reinvent the wheel, the center of dogdom's circle, that great canine mandala, the new hub of my life, the breed that makes other dogs look subcanine, the Alaskan

52

malamute. Pardon the digression.

"My father has a hybrid with him," I said. "He'd be glad to introduce you."

"He already has. Ho."

"Oh."

"Says he lives alone in Maine with nineteen of them. Nineteen wolf dogs. Correct?"

"If he says so. That sounds about right." Buck also had a bitch due in a couple of days, but it seemed better not to mention it. "He's sort of an expert on wolves and dogs," I said. "Especially wolves. He gives talks about it. He was at the Museum of Science a while ago." It's almost as sane and respectable as a golden retriever.

"He invited me to visit," De Franco said. "Said I might like one. He said I might like a wolf." Tap. Tap.

Oh, Buck, if you had to offer him a wild animal, couldn't you have had the sense to make it a reindeer?

"Really? He doesn't usually do that," I said. "They aren't exactly the ideal family pet." My father never, of course, admits that, just that the breeding program isn't too advanced yet, but he never places the pups in families with kids, either.

"He tells me he's working on a strain that will make the perfect hunting dog."

It's nothing more than a harmless effort to combine his hobbies, really, and you should hear the enthusiasm in his voice when he talks about replicating man's earliest interdependent relationship with canines, but I just smiled and passed it off. "A golden retriever is the perfect hunting dog," I said.

"He mentioned golden retrievers, as a matter of fact. He told me your mother lives with hers."

"In a manner of speaking," I said. Oh, hell. The Victorians devoted a lot of time to the question of

53

whether dogs and people go to the same heaven. After Marissa died, my father went through a bad spell. Then he resolved the question. Once he decided that my mother wasn't lonely, he perked up and got his first wolf dog. Lots of people believe that dogs go to heaven. Lord Byron even wrote a poem about it. It just sounds eccentric.

"When did your parents separate?"

"Almost nine years ago."

"He took it hard?"

"Yes. They'd been very devoted." To dogs, of course.

"He hunts?"

"Yes. He lives in Maine. He fishes, too."

"He collects guns. And hunting knives."

"He also collects fishing rods and reels. He ties fishing flies."

De Franco looked straight at me. "He invited me for a meal of sea urchins."

"Eggs," I said. "You eat the eggs, not the whole thing. They're considered to be a delicacy. They're popular in Japan."

De Franco didn't look reassured. "He's described his, uh, meeting with Celia Quigley." Celia, so that was it. De Franco wasn't ho-hoing or tap-tapping anymore.

"I was there," I said, "for some of it."

"He's staying with you?"

I said he was. I never promised to keep him there.

Jolly old De Franco asked me a lot of other questions, too. He asked about Sissy. Did I know her? How well? What time was it when I found her? It seemed to me he knew the answers already. Or else he wasn't very interested in them. He was interested in Buck.

CHAPTER 7

THE ONLY FURTHER COMPETITION AT THE BAYSIDE Exposition Center that day was the contest to see who regretted Sissy's murder most: the exhibitors whose wins wouldn't count, the exhibitors who'd never even entered the ring, or the American Kennel Club and Masconomet Dog Club officials who'd have to handle the complaints and straighten out the paperwork for the aborted show.

We obedience handlers comported ourselves well. We're used to accepting the inevitable. A bitch comes in season the morning of a show, and there's not a damn thing you can do. You could show her in breed, but not obedience. Or two seconds before the end of the long down, when you know that for once you're no more than three or four points away from the legendary two hundred, a perfect score, a static-crackling loudspeaker blasts out a reminder that there's no smoking allowed except in designated areas, and your dog leaps in the air as if he's been caught lighting up.

"I know, I know," Faith said. "It's only a dog show. There'll be others. But what a pain in the neck."

"Shh! The husband is right over there," I said. "He looks pretty upset."

He was emerging from the corridor to the lunch rooms with his son by his side and another man just in back of them—a cop, I guessed. I'd never seen the guy without Sissy before, and without her, he didn't look so weird, just limp and defeated.

"He ought to look relieved. I'm sure she was a big embarrassment to him," Faith said. "You know, she used to say terrible things about me."

55

I didn't think much about it. People who show in breed are always saying terrible things about each other. And complaining that people are telling lies about them.

"Yeah," I said. "You told me."

"And Libby! You wouldn't believe the things she said about Libby."

"I gathered there was a little competition there."

"What there was, was unbelievable jealousy. I mean, how could Sissy really expect to compete? When her husband runs a drugstore, and meanwhile Libby's got a blank check from Mimi Nichols? Look at any of the magazines or newsletters, and you'll see the ads. Thank you, judge so and so. And you can say whatever you want, but the judges do read those, you know. It doesn't hurt."

An ad like that is a full-page spread in one of the breed quarterlies or a magazine that goes to American Kennel Club judges. At the top of the page is a picture taken at a show with the handler, the dog, and the judge, who's smiling and holding the ribbons. Underneath, there's the dog's name in giant boldface print, then maybe a pedigree, then something like "Happydog's Busy Lizzie goes BOS, BOW, 5-point major from Open class. Thanks, Mr. John C. Judge!" When Mimi Nichols hired Libby Knowles to handle the pointers, she'd gotten herself a professional who knew all the tricks and who understood, as Faith said, that the ads don't hurt. What they do is cost.

"And, of course," Faith continued, "Libby can go wherever she wants, and Sissy had to schlep around in a beat-up station wagon and, you know, look for a cheap motel or whatever and hope the car wouldn't break down on the way home. The thing about handling for Mimi Nichols, I guess, is there's no limit. And, furthermore, if you ask me, she has no idea about what handlers normally do and don't do, and Libby has no intention of telling her. If you ask me, she's practically turned it into a full-time job. With a lot of perks. And no limit on anything. Can you imagine? I mean, she literally can pay anything."

"That would be hard to take," I said. "For anyone, not just Sissy. It must've seemed so unfair."

"Life isn't fair."

"Yeah," I said. "What I can't see, though, is how this could have happened here."

"*No* one saw, I think."

"But, look, Faith, there were thousands of people around. How many people were here? How many dogs were registered—nineteen hundred something? I don't know how many people that makes, but if you count all the owners, handlers, spectators? Plus the officials and the people who run the concession stands? How could nobody see?"

"She was probably sneaking a cigarette," Faith said. "She did that all the time. She'd scrunch down between the crates. She was always blowing smoke into the dogs' faces. Besides, this is a dog show. Nobody looks at people."

"*No refund?*" The shouting woman wore a red-flowered dress stretched tightly across a jutting bosom against which she pressed a bewildered-looking Lhasa Apso. "What the hell do you mean, no refund?"

Her target, an elderly man in a gray suit with an official's badge pinned to the lapel, calmly read to her from the show catalog. From the tone of his voice, it was obvious that he'd read the same passage aloud to other disgruntled exhibitors, too. " 'If because of riots, civil disturbances, or acts beyond the control of the

57

management it is impossible to open or to complete the show, no refunds of entry fee will be made.' I'm sorry," he said.

"Twenty dollars for this one and twenty for the bitch!" the woman yelled at him.

"I'm very sorry," he said. "Every show has the same policy."

"Forty dollars! That's not fair."

"Life isn't fair," I told the woman. "It's all a dog show. It's all unfair."

She looked startled.

"Come on, Rowdy," I said. "Let's get out of here."

We did, but not as quickly as I would have liked. Buck, who seldom asks for human help, but occasionally drafts me into service on the grounds that I'm still one of his pups, was taking down his display and packing it up.

"Are you sure this is all right? Aren't you supposed to leave everything the way it is?" I asked.

"They gave up on that and took a lot of pictures," he said. "Realized if they kept all the crates here, it'd mean keeping half the dogs, too."

A lot of people showing more than one dog would have been stuck. Some people would have been able to pile all the dogs into the van or RV or station wagon, but not everyone. Most show dogs are used to riding in crates, and, turned loose, some would have turned on each other.

"Yeah," I said. "I guess. And I suppose people couldn't really leave their stuff, either. I mean, they couldn't be expected to drive back here to pick it up. It would be a nightmare."

If you've never been to a big dog show, you won't believe how much paraphernalia people haul in besides

58

dogs and crates. Someone who'd driven three dogs from New York or New Jersey couldn't drive home with three loose dogs, then show up a week later to retrieve the crates, grooming table, folding chairs, hair dryer, tack box, and cooler, which is some people's idea of the minimum equipment.

"It's a nightmare now," Buck said. "It's terrible. Most peaceful place on God's green earth, a dog show. A little healthy competition, a little petty bickering, you've got to expect that, but not this. Poor silly woman. An ignoramus, of course. You know what she called Clyde?" His big face wrinkled into lines of delight. "Bloodthirsty!"

Clyde had been pacing back and forth at the end of his leash looking uneasy, but at the sound of his name, not the adjective, I assume, he pricked up his ears and stared at my father. A wolf dog looks something like a stretched-out malamute except when you put the two side by side. If you compare them feature by feature, the differences are clear. Rowdy's paws were big, but not compared with Clyde's, and when their mouths were open, you could see that millennia of domestication have miniaturized a wolf's jaws and teeth. Size and anatomy are the last points you'd notice, though. Rowdy's fat, fluffy tail was wagging over his back, his red tongue was sticking out from the big grin on his face, and his warm, happy eyes told you he wasn't scanning for anything more than a friendly pat. Tail down, eyes checking, Clyde looked, as always, serious and watchful. At heart, I thought, Rowdy was a rambunctious clown who took on dignity when circumstances forced it on him, but Clyde's dignity came from the inside and never left him.

Although I suspect that both of them sensed the

59

change in the human atmosphere—the shift from normal show-day anxiety to raw fear—Rowdy's attitude was the same one he expressed whenever a dog fight broke out in his vicinity: delight at the excitement, a determination to force his way into the middle of it, and an unwavering conviction that, whatever happened, he'd end up on top. Rowdy's only fear was that he'd miss out on the fun. If malamutes could speak English, what they'd say is "Me, too! Me, too!" Clyde, however, was showing any sensible wolfs attitude toward trouble. He didn't like it, and he wanted to get away from it.

"Clyde looks nervous," I said to Buck. "Take him home. I'll finish up here."

"He's all right," Buck said. "There's a box of doughnuts around here somewhere. Give him one."

Begging for doughnuts may not seem like dignified behavior, but when Clyde did it, it was. At the sight of the sugary junk in my hand, he rose upright to his full height, perked his ears way up, and tucked in his forepaws to create the effect of a gigantic, eager rabbit, a wolf as cute as a bunny. And he didn't snatch the doughnut and wolf it down, either. I tossed Rowdy the dog biscuit I'd brought along as his reward for a qualifying performance, then held the doughnut out to Clyde. As politely as any cocktail party guest helping himself to a crab meat canapé, Clyde opened those wolf jaws and gently removed the doughnut from my outstretched hand and tossed it down.

"Doughnuts are awful for him, you know," I said to Buck. "You really shouldn't give them to him. But how could you not?"

CHAPTER 8

MY FATHER DOESN'T TRY TO RUN MY LIFE. HE ONLY
wants to offer the guidance and protection he thinks I
need. When puppies grow up, you see, they never
become independent—they're not supposed to—and
Buck still thinks of me as a golden retriever with
unprecedented longevity. If I explain that to Rita, she
narrows her eyes and, for a change, doesn't say
anything. Maybe it's a good thing she was away. I
arrived home to find Buck doing a little more than
guiding things.

Rita was away, but my new tenant, David Shane,
whom Buck had not only met but invited to dinner, was
sitting at the kitchen table. I was glad to see that Buck
evidently approved of him. Kevin Dennehy didn't. He'd
taken one jealous look at Shane and started referring to
him as the Robert Redford of Concord Avenue.

Buck was standing at the stove pontificating about
Irish setters and fishing rods. He was also burning
onions. Why is it that every man who's ever cooked in
my kitchen burns onions? Fortunately, my cream and
terra-cotta color scheme hides the results much better
than the fashionable white most Cambridge types prefer.
I think there's a local ordinance in Cambridge against
nonwhite kitchens, but so far I've escaped the notice of
the authorities.

Buck was making venison stew and feeding meat
scraps to Windy. The prospect, never mind the sight and
odor, of his dog snacking on a dead deer makes the
average Harvard assistant professor violently ill, but
Shane looked not only gorgeous but unnauseated. I

wondered whether he knew what Windy was eating, but the venison was so ripe, the way people like it in Maine, that he could hardly have mistaken it for anything else except equally ripe moose or bear.

"It's been at least two years since I've had venison like this," he said with enthusiasm.

"Oh," I said. "You hunt?"

"A little."

"Is Windy your bird dog? I didn't know that."

"Her? No, she's not trained. I've only had her a couple of months. I'm more of a fisherman, anyway."

"Fishes the Miramichi," Buck said with approval. "The Machias. The Dennys."

Salmon rivers all. Fishing those rivers is more or less the fisherman's equivalent of the stark-white kitchen—a sign of membership in the elite. Fishing for bass is strictly proletarian. It's socially respectable to fish for trout, especially if you're fooling around with your kids or if the salmon aren't running, but in elevated Maine angling circles, you don't even say "fish" unless you mean the Atlantic salmon. What's exclusive about fishing for salmon is that it excludes you from catching fish, or that's my experience. But then again, I'm not much of a fisherman. Furthermore, those jokes about fish stories are no joke to someone who's wasted about a million hours of her life being bored to stupefaction with endless talk about rivers, rods, reels, and dry flies.

"I've had a rough day," I said. "My father must have told you."

Shane had a way of smiling a little while he nodded his head, as if he were saying yes to some totally different, totally intimate question that he understood the way nobody had ever understood that intimate question before.

It wasn't easy to think straight looking at that smile, but I managed to keep cool. "Could I ask you to put Windy upstairs for a while so I can bring Rowdy in and give him his dinner? I can't feed him with another dog around. Where's Clyde?"

Clyde was in the yard. After Shane put Windy in his own apartment and I gave Rowdy his Eukanuba—premium quality, guaranteed thirty percent protein—I excused myself from a deep discussion about Kosmic reels that I expected still to be going on after my shower.

When I finished drying my hair, the kitchen was empty, but I could hear my father's rumbling voice in the hall and Shane's prep school, Ivy League voice answering him. Shane sounded naturally upper crust, not affected, and, in fact, attractive. I hoped Buck wouldn't tell him about any of his recent conversations with my mother. Or her dogs.

I needn't have worried. And everything Buck said about law and order sounded reasonable coming from someone who'd been through what everyone at the dog show had been through that day. Furthermore, although the venison stew would have been better if Buck hadn't burned the onions and the venison hadn't been quite so ripe, it wasn't bad. All in all, the dinner was a big success except that Shane and Buck talked too much about fish and fishing, and for once, it wasn't entirely Buck's fault. Although I gathered that Shane was some kind of biochemist, not an ichthyologist, he had more to say about salmon than anyone except my father would have wanted to hear. It turned out that one of his colleagues was Matt Gerson, a guy I knew from dog training and Buck knew because Matt's an expert on wolves—an expert with academic credentials, unlike

63

my father. The whole evening was such a success that I was surprised at the first thing Buck said after Shane left.

"Your insurance doesn't cover tenants' property, does it?"

"Of course not."

"Good. Make sure you're not responsible."

"Why?"

"Haven't you been up there?"

"Yeah. He's got nice furniture," I said. My father's having noticed seemed out of character. I'd have guessed that he couldn't distinguish between a leather couch and an orange crate.

"What the fellow's got up there is no ordinary collection of fishing gear. Don't you know an old Payne rod when you see one?"

"I know the name," I said. "Does he have one?"

"A museum display," Buck said. "You didn't see the books?"

"Of course I saw books. This is Cambridge. He's an assistant professor."

"Call your insurance company tomorrow. I don't want you responsible."

"Sure," I said. "So what did you think of Windy?"

If you ask Buck a question about an Irish setter, you can expect an answer within seconds, but he paused.

"Pretty," he said. "What's happened to the vet?" he added.

Although I'm not religious in the conventional sense, I do believe that everything is part of an interconnected system. For example, if Sissy had set up in another grooming area at the Masconomet show, the show wouldn't have been canceled, I wouldn't have been exhausted that night, and Clyde would probably have been calm enough to stay in the guest room with Buck. My exhaustion is no excuse. Buck doesn't trust Cambridge, but he knows almost nothing about what is and isn't dangerous or stupid in a city. When Clyde got edgy inside my house and my father wanted to let him spend the night in his van, I should have said it wasn't safe, but all I said was that it wasn't a good idea. In the morning, Clyde was gone.

"Of course I left the windows open," Buck hollered at me. "Did you want him to suffocate?"

We were standing on the sidewalk by his white Chevy van. A bumper sticker on the rear said: "Keep Maine Green. Shoot a Developer."

"You did lock it?" I asked.

"Yes, I locked it." Buck hadn't even washed his face yet. His hair stood up wildly around his big head.

"But you left that side window open?" It's a customized van with a couple of square windows, and the screen of one was torn away. "He was nervous," I added. "It looks to me as if he clawed it open and got out."

My father didn't buy that explanation at all, but was convinced that Clyde had been stolen. I was sorry Rita was away. It seemed to me his worry about Clyde was making him paranoid. At the very least, he took Clyde's disappearance personally and insisted that it had something to do with Sissy Quigley.

"Did I tell you what she called him?" His face was red. "Bloodthirsty."

"Yesterday, you thought that was funny," I said. "Anyway, she said the same thing about Rowdy. And besides, she's dead."

"And," he said, ignoring me, "she lived a block or

two from here. Didn't you tell me that yourself?"

"She's dead," I said again.

"That husband isn't."

"He doesn't even know you. Does he?"

"Oh, he was there, too."

As I learned later, according to every version of the confrontation except Buck's, the husband, Austin Quigley, had tried his hapless best to make his wife and Buck calm down and had finally succeeded in extricating Sissy.

"This is one hell of a fix I'm in," he said, "with Millie due."

Next to Clyde, Millie was Buck's current favorite. She'd been bred to Clyde sixty-one days earlier. The gestation period for wolves and dogs is about sixty-three days, which is why Buck had intended to return to Maine the morning after the show.

"Maybe you can get Regina to stay." Regina Barnes is Buck's wolf-sitter.

"Leaves for her sister's at four today."

"Al?"

"Busy."

"Someone else?"

He'd already checked. Owls Head, Maine, is not large enough to offer an ample supply of people eager to house-and pet-sit for Buck, and even fewer willing to act as midwife to a wolf dog bitch about to deliver her first litter, not that Buck would have trusted anyone except himself.

"You can't leave Millie alone," I said. "Look, I'll find Clyde. I promise."

"God's balls," Buck said.

It was a feeble way to say thanks.

CHAPTER 9

LOSING ANY DOG IS BAD, BUT LOSING A WOLF DOG IS worse. Lots of dog lovers will take in a wandering dog, check his tags, and call the owner, but how many people will take in what looks like a wild animal and is probably so scared that he acts like one, too? In the country, you have to pray that no one shoots him. No matter where you are, you have to hope either that he comes home or that someone mistakes him for a funny-looking German shepherd.

I envied Rowdy's self-confidence, based though it was on a failure to appreciate that anything was wrong. From his viewpoint, we were out for nothing more than a long, long walk, and my whistles and calls were cries of encouragement to him.

"I'm not talking to you, buddy," I told him a couple of times. He didn't believe me.

By the time we got home, Buck's van was gone, but on the kitchen table, he'd left a package clumsily wrapped in the green paper with red bows the Owls Head store carries at Christmastime.

My mother was a meticulously polite person, and once in a while, Buck makes a halfhearted effort to maintain the family standards she set. She must have informed him that it's correct for a houseguest to express his gratitude with a small present. The package was fairly large, and so was the burgundy carrying case inside, but the revolver itself was small, my father's idea of the perfect little hostess gift.

Ladysmith, it was called, a .38 special with a heavy three-inch barrel, but, still, a real lady's weapon—a Smith & Wesson Model 60 Ladysmith, top of the line, with a wood-grained stock and frosted finish on the barrel. Great. With a little effort, I'd be able to find frosted lipstick and nail polish to match. In Massachusetts, the possession of a handgun with no permit carries a mandatory one-year jail sentence. I'd be able to sit in my cell color-coordinating my makeup and manicure with my confiscated revolver. The last time Buck gave me a handgun, I reminded him of that law, but, as usual, he claimed that the U.S. Supreme Court was going to overturn it any day. I also said that with a malamute that looks like Arnold Schwartzenegger disguised as a wolf, I didn't need a gun, but Buck had never heard of Arnold and insisted that a Schwartzenegger was a rare German hunting dog.

I don't like guns, and, as I've said, I don't need a handgun. Even so, as Kevin sometimes reminds me, I'm a country girl at heart. I lifted the little Ladysmith out of its fitted case and held it. I even loaded it. Naturally, ammunition was part of the present. In his own way, Buck is thoughtful. When I was a kid, he always remembered batteries for the battery-operated toys, too. Then I unloaded it, tucked it back in the case, and put the whole thing on the high shelf in my bedroom closet, out of the reach of children.

The Boston *Globe*, like every other newspaper, is usually short of news on Monday. Maybe that's why a dog made the front page, an event that normally happens only when Susan Butcher wins the Iditarod sled dog race, and it happens then only because it's impossible to photograph her without having a dog or two shove its way into the frame, since she owns more than a hundred. Sissy would have hated the photo that went with the story about her. It showed some people I

68

didn't know leading their Afghan hound—not a pointer—out of the back door of Bayside. The people looked disappointed. Sissy would have hated the story itself, too, and not just because it was news of her death. It announced to the world that she was fifty-five years old, first of all, and it never once mentioned pointers, just dogs, as if Max and Lady might equally well have been Cavalier King Charles spaniels or Manchester terriers instead of pointers, as if their breed didn't matter. It had mattered to Sissy. If I die a violent death, I hope the *Globe* gets things straight: "Alaskan Malamute Grieves Owner" or, with luck, "Companion Dog Malamute Suffers Loss."

CHAPTER 10

CAMBRIDGE ANIMAL CONTROL. THE SPCA. THE Animal Rescue League. And the others. I tried them all. Monday. Tuesday. Lost-dog ads in all the papers, the *Globe*, the *Herald*, the *Tab*, the Cambridge *Chronicle*. In the Back Bay lives a woman who takes in stray dogs and places them with families. It's rumored that if she doesn't find enough strays, she creates them, so to speak. If you ever adopt a dog from her, check its tags. No one else may have bothered to call the owners. I called her, and a lot of other people and places, too. The lost-dog signs I posted all over Cambridge had a photo of Clyde that didn't Xerox too badly. The signs said he looked wolflike and acted shy.

Rowdy and I walked so much that I started wearing hiking boots for our expeditions, and I whistled so much that my mouth looked as if I'd been on some kind of fad lemon diet. Even though I always left the answering machine on when we went out, I worried about missing any calls about Clyde, but as soon as we got home, I'd worry about not doing anything active to find him. Most of the messages were from Buck, even though I phoned him a couple of times a day. On Sunday night, he had sounded worried. On Monday, he had sounded angry. By Tuesday, Millie still wasn't in labor, and he was frantic about Clyde, wildly suspicious of Austin Quigley, and insistent that I get in touch with Matt Gerson.

By Tuesday morning, there'd been four messages from Lieutenant De Franco asking Buck and me to return his calls—I had more important things to do—and two messages from Steve asking me to call him,

70

too. I didn't.

The only in I had anywhere was whatever influence I have with Kevin Dennehy, but I probably didn't need it. He'd met Clyde, and he likes dogs, anyway. He had one once, Trapper, but he's refused to get another since Trapper died. He loves dogs too much to have one, or so he says. So don't have one, I always tell him. Have lots and lots.

"I don't like to ask favors," I said when I reached him at the Central Square station on Tuesday morning, "but I need help."

"Has your father left town?"

"He had to. He didn't have any choice." I explained.

"Mickey's just going to love this story," he said when I told him about Millie and said that not even De Franco could expect her to whelp her first litter alone.

"I told him everything I know," I said. "And Buck didn't have anything to do with it. Come on, Kevin. You know that. He was there, but so were a few thousand other people. Where was her husband?"

"With the kid. In the men's room."

"That's a great alibi," I said. "From a nice impartial witness, their son. And furthermore, the bathrooms are right near where it happened, you know."

We talked a little more about Sissy's murder, in which Kevin had a special interest, not just because of De Franco or my father or me but because, to my surprise, Kevin had actually gone in and out of Quigley Drugs without having the sign fall on his head. In other words, he'd been a customer. Since Quigley Drugs was only a couple of blocks from Appleton and Concord— Kevin's is the first house on Appleton—I wouldn't have been surprised except that I'd always assumed that Quigley's didn't have any customers.

71

"It's all right," he said. "It's a regular kind of a place."

Huron Drug, on Huron Avenue, is about the same distance away as Quigley's. I always go to Huron because it has a post office as well as a pharmacy, and dog writers have to make as many trips to the post office as other writers do. I'd never thought of Huron Drug as exclusive, but I suppose that in Kevin's eyes, catering to Brattle Street by carrying imported soaps, loofahs, pumice stones, and English back brushes made it, in contrast to Quigley's, irregular.

Before Kevin hung up, I asked him to put in a word for me with the guys in Animal Control. "You can get them to keep a special eye out for Clyde, right? They can do that. And tell them he's harmless."

"Right," said Kevin. "I'll tell them to watch out for a harmless wolf."

Kevin is mostly bark. I thought he'd help, or at least try. I think he has a slight crush on me. Even so, I didn't ask him to speak to his cousin, not about me, not about my father. It was a subject I preferred to let drop.

My ads and signs offered a reward. The calls started that morning.

"How big was the dog?" I asked a woman in Somerville who thought she might have seen Clyde.

"Why, a little smaller than Billy," she said.

"What kind of a dog is Billy?" I asked.

She laughed. "Billy's not a dog! He's my son."

Billy was four, too small to be bigger than Clyde.

That afternoon while I was whistling and calling up Appleton toward the river, Rowdy and I ran into Mimi Nichols. For once, she was alone and wearing clothing made of an identifiable material, heavy cotton jersey, or at least I think so. I was, of course, walking, but she was really walking. For exercise. In costume. Does Neiman-Marcus sell sweat suits? If so, they're probably called "fitness wear" or something, but the pale gray outfit she had on must have come from there, if not from Bonwit's. And, of course, her shoes were made for aerobic walking, too, not just for putting one foot in front of the other. It's understood in Cambridge that one mile in a suit and shoes like Mimi's is equivalent to ten miles in an old windbreaker, jeans, and hiking boots.

As always, though, she acted lovely and remembered my name.

"This is Rowdy," I said, even though I knew she'd forget his name as soon as we parted ways.

"A husky? Why, he's beautiful!" she exclaimed.

As Libby had said, she didn't know anything about dogs. First of all, a Siberian husky is called a Siberian, not a husky, and, second, as you already know, Rowdy wasn't one.

"Thank you," I said, anyway, and after I explained about malamutes, I told her about Clyde, who might wander her way. In terms of property values, her neighborhood, just off Brattle Street, is two million dollars up from mine, but geographically, it's two or three blocks.

"That's terrible," she said. She sounded as if she meant it. "What can I do?" she added, half to herself, and I realized that she was used to being asked for help, preferably in three figures or more. "Reggie," she said. "He's wonderful about things like this. He can do anything. I don't think he has any strays now, but sometimes he finds lost dogs. He finds families for them."

Rowdy and I followed Mimi down her driveway to the back of the house, where an addition had expanded a mere twenty or so rooms to at least thirty, not counting the four long concrete-paved dog runs or the big exercise pen with its own cedar-shingled doghouse. I've mentioned Cambridge real estate? If Mimi ever found herself short of funds, I thought, she could move out the pointers and get six or eight hundred a month each for their apartments.

Sunshine and another male stood barking in their runs. The second one was called Regis, I learned later, and he'd been Ed Nichols's hunting dog. In the big exercise pen, a third pointer, a runty-looking bitch, ran up to the gate, trembled all over, and urinated. Rowdy was lunging at the end of his lead, giving the males a suitably top-dog greeting while not missing the chance to take advantage of the poor bitch's pathetic submission by frightening her almost to death.

"We have this trouble with Zip in the house," Mimi said apologetically. I could hardly hear her over the din. "Libby says she can't help it. She's working on it. We don't show her."

Libby had been tactful. Maybe, just maybe, with endless patience Libby might be able to cure the submissive urination—that's what it's called—but not poor Zip's cow hocks, undershot bite, or pigeon breast.

Mimi must have read my face. "I bought her myself," she added, "from a pet shop. She has papers." Having papers means nothing, of course. Take one look at Zip. "Regis was my husband's hunting dog, and after Ed died, I started to keep him in the house, for company. And then one day, just on impulse, I thought he ought to have a companion, and I ran out and got Zip. It's not the kind of thing I usually do."

"How did you find Libby?" I asked, mostly to curb my impulse to deliver a lecture on the evils of pet shops, and I mean evils. I won't buy so much as a collar or leash from a pet shop that sells puppies. "Rowdy, cut it out. Hush."

"My father found her," Mimi said. "She was at Westminster, and somebody there recommended her." Westminster is to dog shows what the Kentucky Derby is to horse races. "I knew I needed help with Zip, and she is much, much better, and Reggie's wonderful with her, too. Libby's around somewhere. Libby?"

Libby, followed by Reggie, appeared from a door at the back of the house. Although they both had their shirts tucked in and their jeans zipped, I had the impression that our voices and the dogs' barking had roused them from bed and the simultaneous impression that Mimi didn't realize it.

I'd only heard Reggie speak a couple of times before, but I'd suspected real Down East Maine, Hancock County or Washington County, north of Ellsworth and Bar Harbor, north of where the tourists all stop, and I turned out to be right.

"You're from Maine," I said after we all greeted each other.

"Born in Pembroke," he said. That's Washington County. "One godforsaken hole. You never heard of it."

"Oh, yeah? It's near Dennysville," I said. "I've even been to the reversing falls. Twice. But I only saw them reverse once."

He laughed. "Never been there," he said. "I grew up in Machias." His good, solid laugh matched his looks but showed something I wasn't surprised to see in a young guy who'd grown up where he had: teeth too even and white to be real. He was lucky to have any teeth, even false ones. Washington County is rugged, wild, and beautiful, with deep woods too thick to walk

75

through and blueberry barrens that justify the name, a genuine frontier, and it's poor beyond poor. The principal source of income there must be welfare, supplemented by whatever people can eke out packing sardines, raking blueberries, and making Christmas wreaths, none of which leaves a lot over for an orthodontist or even a plain dentist.

Mimi explained about Clyde. After everyone sympathized, Reggie asked a lot of questions about what Clyde looked like, how he acted, where he might be likely to go. He seemed to be the first person besides Buck and me who really understood how bad it was to have Clyde gone and who'd join my effort to find him. Anyone who makes it from Washington County, Maine, to just off Brattle Street—even to the back of a house just off Brattle—is a survivor, I thought, and a good ally. Besides, he made a big fuss over Rowdy, who sat up, put his paws in Reggie's hands, and licked his face.

CHAPTER 11

S<small>HORTLY AFTER</small> I <small>RETURNED FROM</small> M<small>IMI'S</small>, D<small>E</small> F<small>RANCO</small> showed up at my door.

"Ho-ho," he said. "Been out a lot? You've been hard to find lately."

"Yeah. Trying to find a lost dog. Come in."

Old reliable, my ferocious guard dog, pushed his way past me, sniffed De Franco's crotch, and dropped onto the linoleum. Then he rolled onto his back and wiggled his legs in the air.

"He turned up, huh?"

"No. Actually, it's my father's dog that's lost."

"Didn't know he had dogs."

I ignored the dig.

"The one he had at the show," I said. "The wolf dog. Clyde. He's a hybrid. Kevin's helping look for him." The reference to Kevin was supposed to suggest legitimacy. "Have a seat."

"Thanks. Probably stolen," De Franco said.

Right jolly old elf.

"Big market," he went on.

"Is there?"

"Flashy dog, kid maybe struts around with it, gets sick of it, sells it."

"Where?"

"Labs."

"Labs?" Run that through my mental word processor and what you get first is Labrador retriever, but I remembered our last board meeting. "Laboratories?"

"Yeah. Aren't you the dog expert? Tell me about scissors for dogs."

77

"I don't know much about them."

"More than I do."

"They're called grooming shears," I said. "What do you want to know?"

"Who uses them. What kind. What for. Big ones, we're talking about. Eight and a half inches long."

"Okay," I said. "I don't know a whole lot about grooming, but, for one thing, you're right. That's big. I'm no expert on grooming, but I'm pretty sure you wouldn't use those except on one of the long-haired breeds, something with a really long, thick coat."

"So basically, you use these for a haircut? What about on their claws?"

"No."

"Never?"

"Never. For that you use nail clippers. Nobody'd trim nails with a pair of shears. For one thing, you couldn't, physically. Dogs' nails are too thick. Rowdy, sit. Give your paw."

Giving his paw had always been one of Rowdy's favorite tricks, mostly because it was an excuse to hold hands. Hold paws. Whichever it is. He plunked himself down between my chair and De Franco's and lifted his right forepaw. I held it, pressed gently on the pad, and spread the toes.

"See? When you trim the nails, all you take off is the end. His nails don't need trimming now, but if they did, they'd be long, and you'd see hooks on the ends. You'd want to cut off the hooks, and a pair of shears would be too big. They'd get in the way, and dogs' nails aren't like human nails, anyway. They're really hard, more like bone, sort of soft bone." I'm so used to talking about dogs that it didn't register until I heard myself say it. If those shears hadn't gone through bone, they must

78

have gone between it, between her ribs, soft bone. "Oh, God. That's what happened to Sissy."

"Yeah. That's why I'm here." He sounded gentle and serious, not like the silly caricature he liked to make of himself. For the first time, I could see him as a relative of Kevin's.

"I know," I said. "Jesus. Look, let's get this out in the open. My father's a character. He has odd interests. Hobbies. And where he comes from, you know, they aren't all that odd. But, honest to God, he wouldn't hurt anyone."

"Yeah," De Franco said. "Dennehy says he's an odd duck but he's harmless."

"That's true," I said.

"And a Miss Barlow says she was talking to him when the murder occurred."

"Faith?"

"You know her?"

"Yeah. She was going to show Rowdy for me. She has malamutes. So she was with Buck?"

"Yeah. A couple of people confirm it. The point is, I need information. Mrs. Quigley had dogs with short hair. She had pointers. Tell me why she would have had those shears. Or who else would've."

"They weren't hers," I said. "I thought you knew that."

He didn't say anything.

"They originally belonged to Libby," I said. "She handles for Mimi Nichols."

"Libby Knowles."

"Yeah. Look, Libby isn't the only one who's told me this. The story is that Sissy stole things. Or that's what people say. Mostly, from what I've heard, she was—I guess you'd call it light-fingered. She lifted unimportant

79

stuff. And maybe she didn't know what those shears were worth. She probably just thought they were ordinary grooming shears. They were out of her price range. Libby says they cost close to three hundred dollars."

"To cut a dog's hair?" He sounded incredulous.

"I know. It seems outrageous to me, too, but remember who Libby works for."

"Yeah," he said.

If solid gold were hard enough to make good shears, Mimi Nichols would have been able to afford it, of course. As it was, she could have paid for Geib shears more easily than Libby could have, even working for her. Maybe the shears had actually been Mimi's. But that made no sense. Groomers and handlers provide their own equipment. And why would anyone—Mimi, Libby—have bought giant shears like that to groom a pointer? At most, you'd need a pair of smallish, curved, blunt-end scissors, I thought, to trim the whiskers or the hair on the feet. It made no sense at all. But Mimi Nichols wasn't, after all, Libby's first or only client.

"They must have been in Sissy's tack box," I said. "You know what that is? It's what you keep grooming equipment in. You must've seen it. It'd have brushes, combs, nail clippers, spray bottles, chalk white, a whole lot of stuff like that."

"Disposable gloves."

"Oh. Yeah, maybe."

"Not standard equipment?"

"Not really. Maybe for Sissy, though, because of her allergies. She told me she was allergic to dogs, and lots of people react to the sprays and grooming powders, too. But at shows, maybe you should know, one thing professional handlers do is dress up. And amateurs showing their own dogs in breed do, too. You know what that means? In breed? Not in obedience?"

"Yeah."

"People who are showing in obedience don't usually get all dressed up, but if you're showing in breed, you do. Men wear suits, most of the time, and the women practically all wear dresses or skirts, and some of them get really dressed up. Naturally, if you groom a dog, you'll be covered with fur and grooming spray and stuff, so the men don't put on their suit jackets until just before they go into the ring, and some of the women wear smocks or something. Anyway, one thing the gloves would do is protect your hands, so you don't spoil your nails."

"Her fingernails were plastic. She sold cosmetics."

"She used a lot. Obviously, she wanted to look young."

"I know," he said.

"She didn't, though. She just looked sad."

As soon as De Franco left, I paid a visit to Quigley Drugs, mostly to assuage Buck. On the street in front of the store, Pete Quigley, Sissy's infant-faced son, was just getting into the old green station wagon. I walked up to the car.

"Pete? I'm Holly Winter."

He didn't seem to recognize me, and it seemed awkward to remind him of where and when we'd met.

"You need something done?" he asked. I didn't know what he meant.

"I wanted to say I'm sorry about your mother. I knew her a little."

"Oh," he said. "Yeah." He sounded as if he'd either forgotten her or forgotten that she'd died. He finished stepping into the car, slammed the door, and drove away.

Austin Quigley, who stood behind the counter at the back of the store, didn't look as if he'd forgotten, and looked pretty sad, worse than sad, but his pharmacist's coat was white and starched. From the inside, Quigley Drugs was better than I'd expected, not like Huron, but clean, except for the front windows. The Quigleys had made a recent effort to modernize. The linoleum, beige with mud-colored flowers, was new, and so were the plastic counters and the rows of cheap, half-empty metal-edged shelves, but everything was displayed too far apart in a failing effort to create the impression of ample stock. To fill my hands, I picked up a bottle of hydrogen peroxide, which is good for cleaning dogs' ears.

"May I help you?" he asked in a monotone.

Sure. My father wants to know whether you stole his wolf.

"My name is Holly Winter. We've met before." At your wife's murder. Did you do it? "I train dogs."

His face showed what I assumed was recognition.

"I'm so sorry about Sissy," I said.

He looked hurt. "I can't close the store. I have to stay open. People rely on us," he said.

"Of course."

"You don't want cosmetics, do you?"

"No. Not today."

"Because she did all that. I don't know what I'm going to do. My wife was a trained cosmetician, you know. I don't know anything about it. Foundation, blush, all of it?" For a second, he sounded almost frivolous, or maybe just on the edge of hysteria. "I don't know how I'm going to manage, and the register, too,

82

she did that, and the books. And she was very good with customers, always asking people how they were, being friendly, all that."

"I'm really sorry," I said.

"And Pete's useless. A useless good-for-nothing. In the store, he's useless. Two weeks of pharmacy school, and he was back home, and now he's taken up painting and wouldn't even give his mother a hand behind the register."

"Painting?"

"Houses." The image of Pete at an easel must have tickled him. He started to giggle. What was the right thing to do for hysteria? Slap him? Run outside for the sprinkler again?

"I need some toothpaste, too," I said. It was the first thing I spotted. Could anyone have hysterics while selling Colgate? "And this bottle of peroxide."

Suddenly, he turned coy. He smirked and cocked his head. "I'll bet you use that for your dog's ears, don't you?" he said as if he were being clever and charming.

"Yes," I said. "Speaking of dogs, my father's dog got lost near here sometime Sunday night. Or early Monday morning. A big dog. He looks like a wolf."

He shook his head. I paid him, and he put the toothpaste and peroxide in a white bag that didn't even have Quigley Drugs printed on it.

"If you happen to see a dog like that, could you let me know? It's possible he's around here somewhere. I live at the corner of Appleton and Concord, in the red house. I'm on the first floor."

"My wife was the dog person," he said. "I was never any good with them. Oh, I tried, all that heel, stay—but I never could get them to listen to me."

The past tense set my nerves on edge. "You've still

83

got them, don't you?" I asked.

"Oh, Max is still out there," he said.

"Lady?"

"Bit me yesterday. Got my calf. She sank her teeth right in. I had to take her right to the vet."

"Was she hurt?"

He gave me a big smile.

"Had to put a needle to her," he said cheerfully. "Bit me. Like I told you, right on the calf. I didn't have any choice, did I?"

Love hungry and frightened, Lady might have bitten him out of fear, but she'd been a good pointer, just a needy one, not a physical and neurotic wreck like Mimi's poor pampered Zip, and for some reason, I'd liked her. No, not Steve, I thought. Let it be some other vet who did it. Any other vet. Not Steve.

"What vet do you use?" I asked. I had to know.

"That young one who took over from Dr. Draper. Dr. Delaney."

Delaney. Steve Delaney. The conscientious vet. The murdering bastard.

When I got home, my machine had a message from Steve. I called his home number, got his machine, and left a message of my own. As soon as I hung up, the phone rang.

CHAPTER 12

"HOLLY? AL BARNES."

Some elderly and not-so-elderly residents of Owls Head, Maine, holler into the phone, but Al doesn't. Al's sister, Regina, is Buck's usual house-and dog-sitter. She doesn't like me any better than she liked my mother. I don't even think she knows the difference; when she speaks to me at all, she calls me Marissa. But Al has always been a friend of the family's. He's at least ten years younger than his sister, in his early seventies, and sharp. He's an old fishing and hunting buddy of Buck's.

"Hi, Al."

"Holly, I thought you ought to know. I'm kind of worried about your father." Not much worries Al.

"What's the problem?"

"Well, I think he ain't slept since he got back. I hate to say it, but I think he ain't right in the head." This from a man who gives every indication of thinking that Regina is right in the head.

"He's worried about Clyde," I said. "You know Clyde's lost? And he's probably sitting up with Millie, waiting for her to go into labor."

"Holly, he's in the barn, crying like a baby, and he won't let me in. I been out every chance I get, and I pound on the door, but he won't open it."

Buck had sounded bad on the phone, but not that bad.

"Damn," I said. "I'd leave this minute, but he'll have a fit if I show up there. There's no guarantee he'd let me in, anyway. I promised him I'd find Clyde, and as soon as I do, he'll be all right. And, look, I think once Millie's labor starts, he'll pull himself together."

Al keeps going by driving the school bus, digging clams, pumping gas, taking care of people's summer cottages, and doing at least a dozen other jobs, all of them legal. Those summer places that stand empty from Labor Day to Memorial Day offer certain tempting employment opportunities that not everyone resists, but Al's an honest guy. I believed him when he assured me he'd do his best to keep checking on Buck, but I knew he didn't have a lot of free time. Furthermore, he couldn't solve Buck's problems. Only Clyde's return and Millie's labor could do that.

On the chance that someone had mistaken Clyde for a funny-looking malamute, I called Faith Barlow. Some breeders don't want anything to do with rescue work. For one thing, the average breeder has too many dogs already and doesn't necessarily have room for more, especially dogs that could bring fleas, mange, and diseases into the kennel. Also, the dogs turned over to shelters and humane societies tend to be pet shop dogs, not prime specimens of the breed, and they may have had nasty temperaments to begin with or lives that would make any dog turn mean. Once in a while, though, Faith will take one in, but only a malamute, of course.

I got her answering machine. The tape started with woo-wooing malamutes. Then Faith's voice said, "Hi, this is Faith. Sorry, no one's home but the dogs, and we haven't had time to train them to answer the phone yet, but if you'll leave your name and number, we'll call back as soon as possible." Some mals woo-wooed again, and after the beep, I left a message telling her about Clyde and asking her to call. Then I called Buck and got his machine. "This is Buck Winter. Leave a message and one of us will call you," his voice said. A

86

recording of Clyde's beautiful, clear howl sounded. I remembered him standing upright in his giant-rabbit pose, waiting for that doughnut. I didn't leave a message. I couldn't say anything.

By then, late Tuesday afternoon, I'd almost given up the hope that Clyde would wander back to my door or that I'd find him trotting through the neighborhood, but the walking and whistling and calling at least gave me the illusion that I was doing something to locate him, and Rowdy was happy to tag along. When we got out the back door, Kevin was standing on the sidewalk. He had on baggy gray sweatpants and a Cambridge YMCA T-shirt. He was talking to Shane, who had wild Irish Windy at the end of a lead.

"Holly," Kevin called. "How ya doing?"

"I've been better, Kevin," I said. "Hi, Shane."

"I've got some not-so-good news for you," Kevin said. "Couple of other dogs disappeared around here Sunday night, both out of yards."

"Animal Control didn't tell me that," I said.

Kevin just shrugged. "Keep the dogs with you. Or inside. Don't leave them in the yard."

"Of course not," Shane said. I'm sure Kevin didn't like his tone or, for that matter, his voice, accent, clothes, educational background, profession, blond hair, brown eyes, or one single other thing about him.

"We'll be careful," I said. "Is this the first time? I mean, has there been a lot of it lately? Have there been any other dogs stolen in Cambridge?"

"Happens from time to time. We don't always hear about it.

Yes, I thought. And you don't always do anything about it, either. It does happen. A long time ago, it happened to Susan Butcher, who grew up in Cambridge, where she had a Siberian husky stolen. Now she and her Alaskan huskies live not far below the arctic circle, in the land where men are men, and women like Susan Butcher often win the Iditarod sled dog race—in other words, where women are winners and men are sore losers. From what I've read, though, she's still angry about one loss—that stolen dog.

"Maybe you don't always hear about it, Kevin, but you heard about Clyde," I said.

"Holly, I'm real sorry." Kevin looked at his shoes instead of at me.

"Then help me."

"I'm doing my best."

"Are you?"

"Yeah, I am. See you later."

Kevin ran off. My father had locked himself in the barn and was crying. Steve had killed Lady just because that was his job. But Shane was right there with me, not taking off or sobbing or murdering love-hungry pointers.

"Let's take a walk," he said.

Windy's head and tail were a little lowered, and Rowdy was sniffing her with approval. As I may have mentioned, malamutes can act rambunctious and somewhat aggressive with other dogs, but Rowdy just plain liked Windy, who accepted him as top dog but didn't grovel. She wasn't afraid of him.

I needed the walk, and although I don't usually spill personal stuff to people I don't know well, it did me good to talk about everything. I didn't say anything about Steve—I never mentioned his existence—but I told Shane the rest of the story.

"So your father went through an episode like this after your mother died?" he said.

"Worse than this. That's what I'm worried about. I wish Millie would hurry up."

"She was mated to Clyde?"

"Yeah. This is her first litter."

"Clyde's a beautiful animal," Shane said. "These hybrids are fascinating. Your father's quite a guy. I enjoyed meeting him."

"He's a real character." I'm used to explaining him to people.

"A genuine individualist."

"Yes," I said.

"A prototype."

The word impressed me, even though he might just as well have said that when they made Buck they'd broken the mold, hardly a new observation. Maybe I'm easily impressed. I'm definitely not hard to take out to dinner, either. Shane took me to a now-defunct place near Kendall Square called the Daily Catch, which was the best restaurant in Cambridge. A Chihuahua couldn't make it through the day on what most Cambridge restaurants serve for a three-course meal. If you ate at the Daily Catch, you smelled like squid, garlic, and olive oil for a week afterward, but that's how long it took you to feel hungry again, too.

"That venison was a treat," Shane said.

We were sitting opposite each other, reading our menus. Perhaps I should point out that the Daily Catch wasn't a romantic setting unless your idea of romance is blue and white tile, crowds, adequate lighting, and an Italian-looking waiter who doesn't announce that he'll be your waiter tonight when it's obvious that he already is.

"Did you really like it?" I asked.

"Loved it."

"I thought the onions were burned."

"Browned," he said.

"It's nice of you to say that."

As I've explained, the onions were unmistakably burned. I tend to be bluntly truthful myself. Even so, I am embarrassed to say that for most of the meal, we talked about me. Maybe I was too strung out to notice or too flattered to mind. The man was a good listener. It was one of his charms. He had others. More than anyone should. He admired my hair. He'd never known a dog writer before. Wasn't it an interesting occupation? How did I eat so much and stay so thin? Not too thin, of course. How many dogs had I owned? What were they like?

On the way out, we ran into Matt Gerson and his wife, Marty. I'd known that Matt and Shane were in the same department, but during the entire meal, I hadn't asked Shane one question about himself or his work, so it wasn't surprising that we hadn't talked about Matt. Matt and my father know each other because in their own ways, they're both experts on wolves. Incidentally, Matt Gerson looks nothing like a wolf, and neither Matt nor Marty looks like a German shepherd, which is what they had when Matt trained with the Cambridge Dog Training Club. Actually, the Gersons look remarkably like each other, about five six, robust, with wavy brown hair, his on the long side for a man, hers on the short side for a woman. Her voice is deep, his tenor. In other words, they look and sound like married twins.

The Gersons were good friends of mine until we had a silly falling-out, a misunderstanding. When they got a new German shepherd, I showed up with a chew toy for the puppy and a roast chicken for them so they wouldn't have to cook for themselves, but last year, when their baby was born, I forgot to send a card, and their feelings were hurt. I missed them. I should have called, especially because I'd heard that their dog died. But the Gersons don't hold grudges. They greeted me in a friendly way, asked about Buck, heard about Clyde, and told me to visit soon. To avoid stirring up any of the old hard feelings, I didn't offer my condolences about their dog. I would have had to ask about the baby first, and I had forgotten not only its name but its gender, too. They didn't seem to notice. The only coldness they showed, it seemed to me, was toward Shane. I had the impression that while I was crazy about him, they weren't. I thought he was charming. They didn't. Nothing more. No man ever pleases all your friends. For instance, Rita used to go out with a guy I couldn't stand. He thought that dogs were so unsanitary that he wouldn't let Rita touch him after she'd patted Groucho unless she washed her hands first.

As I was stepping out of the Mercedes onto my driveway, with Shane holding the door open for me, Steve Delaney drove by on Appleton Street. I hoped he saw Shane, me, and the Mercedes. I wished Windy had been there for him to see, too.

CHAPTER 13

THAT WAS TUESDAY. ON WEDNESDAY MORNING, Libby Knowles called to tell me that Reggie was doing his best to find Clyde but hadn't had any luck so far. She also asked if I wanted to buy a new printer.

"Mine isn't wonderful, but it works," I said. "What kind?"

"It's supposed to be a good one."

"What does that mean? Laser?"

"Yes."

"How much is it?"

"Cheap."

"How cheap is cheap?"

"Four hundred dollars."

"Used?"

"Practically new."

The price wasn't just low. It was way too low. "When did you start selling printers?" I asked.

"I'm not. I just heard about this, and I thought of you. I know you use a computer."

"Every day." Except for the past few days.

"Where did you hear about this?"

"Somebody told me. If you're not interested, forget it. I was trying to do you a favor."

"Thanks. I'll think it over."

"Hey, do you think you could do me a favor?"

"Sure. What?"

"Could you ask what's-his-name, that cop on your block, about my shears?"

"Kevin. I guess so. Libby, are you sure you really want them back? Why do you want them?"

"They're mine," she said. "They'll have to give them back sometime, won't they?"

I nearly reminded her that, as far as I knew, she hadn't even asked De Franco for them. It seemed to me that I was the one who'd told him they were hers—she hadn't—but I thought she might not like it.

"I don't know," I said. "Probably not for a long time, anyway. They *are* evidence. Hey, how well do you know Sissy's husband? Austin?"

"A little."

"From shows?"

"And the drugstore. I used to go there."

"Do you know what he did? I can hardly believe it. He had one of her dogs destroyed."

"Max!"

"No. The bitch, Lady. He says she bit him."

"Bull!"

"She could have nipped him, maybe," I said.

"Even so! How could he do that?"

"I don't know. He told me himself. I didn't know what to say. If it hadn't been too late, I would've tried to do something."

"I can't believe it," Libby said. "He always just struck me as kind of a nobody. I felt kind of sorry for him, stuck with Sissy. I figured she'd finally pushed him to the limit, you know? There's only so much a person could take of her, if you know what I mean."

"Yeah," I said. I'd had the same idea.

"But Lady? Lady never did him any harm. You know, that is one thing I cannot stand. People just don't like the dog, or they get another one they like better, or whatever, and half the time, they don't even bother to try to give it away."

"I know."

"And a lot of breeders aren't a whole lot better."

"I don't think that's true."

"Yes, it is. They just don't talk about it. Their attitude is, once a dog isn't fit to show anymore, he isn't fit for anything, and they don't want to have to pay the food and vet bills. And it doesn't have a damn thing to do with who can afford it and who can't. If you ask me, half the time they're just lazy. Take one look at a puppy and see he's got some little fault, and do they bother to find a pet home? Oh, no. They're not raising pets. Right?"

"Sometimes."

"And don't tell me your malamute people don't do it."

"Really, Libby, if you're talking about Janet Switzer, you're wrong." Janet is Rowdy's breeder.

"I'm not," Libby said. "I'm not talking about Janet."

"If you mean Faith Barlow," I said, "I don't believe it." I didn't. What Libby said about Faith wasn't true, but it does show you how some dog people talk.

According to Libby, you couldn't blame Austin Quigley for ridding himself of an insufferable wife, but having a dog destroyed was unforgivable. Don't look at *me*. I didn't say it; she did. No matter what the wife was like, nobody had the right to kill her. Fine. But what about Lady? To rid yourself of a dog, all you need to do is pay your money and sign a form stating that you understand that euthanasia isn't reversible. Laughable? Grotesque? True. I've signed those forms. I signed one for Vinnie, my last golden, the day I met Steve Delaney. I should have known then that death was his specialty. But I didn't regret what I'd done for Vinnie. All I did was what I would have wanted a friend to do for me. I'm sorry she had cancer. I'm sorry she died. I'm not sorry I spared her the pain.

Vinnie was old. The Gersons' dog wasn't, just horribly sick, and I hadn't even called them then. In fact, I'd been a rotten friend, and not just about the dog. About the baby, too. Besides, I'd promised Buck I'd ask Matt Gerson about Clyde, just on the off chance that a wolf expert might hear of a wandering wolf, I guess.

Since Matt and Marty look so much like each other, the baby, true to type, looked exactly like both of them, a stocky little thing with their wavy brown hair. He had one of those *J* names, Jason, Joshua, Justin, something like that. He liked the overdue baby present I brought for him, a stuffed animal, a toy malamute. There's an equally cute stuffed wolf, but, considering Matt, I assumed the baby already had five or ten of them already. I was right. When Matt and Marty put the baby to bed soon after I arrived, I saw the pack of toy wolves lined up on a shelf in the nursery, and I was careful not to admire them more enthusiastically than I admired Jason or whatever his name was.

If you watch television, you probably have an image of a professor's big Victorian house filled with upholstered armchairs, shiny tables, crystal, and Bokhara rugs, fire blazing on the hearth, eminent scholar sitting at an oak rolltop desk, the whole bit. Unfortunately for Matt, he's the real thing, not a TV professor, and Marty writes novels, serious books about people, and since she's a real writer, not like me, she earns even less than I do. They own a house in Cambridge, a wood-frame one like mine, but it has only two apartments. The one they live in (painted entirely white, of course) doesn't even have a fireplace, and the furniture consists mostly of director's chairs and a couple of desks made from doors set on sawhorses. The tables shine because they're plastic. Even so, the place is anything but empty. Everywhere you look are brick and board shelves filled with thousands of books, journals, stacks of reprints, and funny objects the Gersons have trash-picked. The kitchen walls are covered with battered lemon squeezers, graters, garlic presses, and patent cooking gadgets whose purpose the Gersons are always trying to guess. The pictures are, of course, photos and posters of wolves, except for some Woolworth-framed mounted displays of the fishing flies Matt ties. Matt doesn't hunt, but in other respects, he's what Buck calls a regular enough guy for a Harvard professor. Fly tying is an art—I'm not kidding—and Matt is a master. The elaborate concoctions of feathers, shiny material, and colored threads are more than just fishing lures—they're a form of highly structured creative expression. Not for the first time, I admired the display.

"That one's such an old-timer, even I know what it is," I said. "It's a Jock Scott. And that one's a Silver Doctor."

"I am impressed." Matt was only half kidding.

"What's that fluffy one?"

"A Gray Hackle Dry," Matt said, "but I didn't tie it. Ed Nichols tied that one."

"Really? I didn't know you knew him. I met his wife the other day, or his widow, I guess I should say. So you knew him?"

"Yes," Matt said.

"Cambridge." Marty smiled. It's such a small world that no one bothers to say so.

"Actually, we both used to fish the Dennys," Matt said.

"Really? Shane did, too," I said. "I think he still does. So Ed Nichols tied that himself?"

"Yeah," Matt said. "Does it look like someone else's?"

"How would I know? No. I thought maybe someone else did, that he had it tied for him. Or he could've bought it."

"Not a chance," Matt said. "Ed tied it. We used to trade. So what's going on?"

After we did some catching up, I raised the subject of Clyde.

"Your father hates to hear this," Matt said, "but I'm convinced that this hybridizing is misguided. It's a mistake. I've said the same thing in print."

"I agree with you," I said. "I've got a malamute now. That's my idea of a wolf dog."

We talked about malamutes, and I asked whether the Gersons were thinking about another dog. They'd decided to wait until what's-his-name was a little older.

"The fence is still up, and the doghouse is still sitting out there," Marty said. "One of these days. We talk about it."

"What are you thinking about getting?" I asked. "Another shepherd?"

"We've been talking about a golden, maybe," Mart said, "or some kind of setter."

"Have you seen Shane's?" I felt compelled to keep speaking his name. Infatuation is impossible to keep secret. "He's got a lovely Irish setter bitch," I went on. "Really lively and really gentle. One like that would be perfect with kids. I don't know where he got her."

The Gersons exchanged identical glances, but neither of them said anything.

"I could ask him," I said.

"Have you been seeing a lot of him?" Matt asked.

"Not a lot. Some. He's my tenant. He's got the third floor."

"Has he been there long?" Matt asked.

"No. He just moved in. Windy, the setter, is just beautiful. You'd love her. I'll find out where he got her. Or you ask him. You're in the same department. You see each other there?"

"From time to time," Matt said. "He also does some work in the private sector."

Private sector. So that explained it. In Matt's view, Shane had sold out to industry, and whatever he did there must be applied, not theoretical, which in Cambridge means that it was lucrative but not classy. I'd wondered how Shane could afford the rent, the clothes, the furniture, the antique fishing gear Buck had admired. Now I knew. But he paid a price. Matt and Marty's hand-picked, trash-picked found objects, their mountains of battered paperbacks, their near-antique Volvo that doesn't always start in the rain? In Cambridge, all that is classier than Mimi Nichols's thirty-room house. And Matt had just had a book accepted by Harvard University Press. In Cambridge, that means he outclassed almost everyone except the other people also published by Harvard University Press, all of whom, were outclassed only by the people published by Oxford University Press. Poor Shane. He had the audacity not only to work for money but to work for a lot of it.

CHAPTER 14

MY FAVORITE COOKBOOK COMES FROM THE Elizabeth H. Brown Humane Society in Orleans, Vermont. It has recipes for dog food, cat food, and people food. It's sometimes hard to tell who's supposed to eat what. Want an easy recipe for homemade dog biscuits? Here's an adaptation. Mix three tablespoons of oil with a third of a cup of water. Mix one cup of whole wheat flour with a quarter cup of soy flour. Stir in the water mixture, roll the dough out, cut it into cookies, and bake at three-fifty until brown. If you want professional results, you can buy bone-shaped cutters, but I just use an upended glass, which is probably why Kevin Dennehy didn't recognize what was cooling on the cake rack that Thursday morning. Kevin must have stupendously strong dental work, and if he had any tartar before, he didn't afterward.

"You were at Quigley's the other day, weren't you?" he said.

"Yeah."

"Stay away from there for now. Don't go back."

"I wouldn't dream of it," I said. "Do you know, I think Austin Quigley is crazy? Or he's going crazy? The man is literally unstable. One second you think he's one person, then a second later, he's totally different. I don't think I've ever seen anybody really have hysterics, but I thought he was going to. He started to giggle. And then I found out he killed one of Sissy's dogs. He actually told me, as if there was nothing wrong with doing it. I don't trust him at all."

"And if you're thinking of having any painting done,

99

do it yourself."

"I always do," I said. "Inside and outside. Why?"

"Pete Quigley does a lot of work around here. He's a house painter."

"I know," I said. "Austin was telling me about it."

"It's not what he calls it," Kevin said. His face was deadpan.

"Who?"

"Pete," Kevin said. "The painter."

"What does he call it?"

"Doing finishes. He's what they call upscale." Kevin was delighted. "He doesn't paint. He applies finishes. Took Mickey an hour to figure out what the guy did for a living."

"Ho," I said. "I'm sorry. He's your cousin, and he's really all right. He drops that Santa stuff after a while."

"You've never heard him in December," Kevin said. "Anyway, I know Rita's away, and I wanted to pass the word to you in case you decided to do some redecorating while she's gone. I don't want him in here."

"It never even occurred to me. Why would I hire someone when I can do it myself?" In a way, Buck is right. My mother didn't really die. Sometimes she speaks through me. "Rita's place doesn't need painting, anyway, and I touched up the third floor while it was vacant."

"Good."

"Look," I said. "I've more or less been assuming Austin had had all he could take. Right? That's what everybody thinks. So now you're telling me it was the kid?" The "kid," I should add, was about my age. "Or he might have? Do you really think he murdered his mother?"

100

"Of course not," Kevin said. "Why, who'd ever do a thing like that? We'd have to invent a new word for it. Let's see. Matricide." He sounded out the syllables. "Would that do?"

"Be serious. Do you think he did it? Does De Franco think so?"

"He thinks they're both weird," Kevin said.

"Genius runs in your family?" I said. "So what's this about?"

"I don't trust your judgment," he said. "That's what it's about."

With no success, I tried to get him to tell me what De Franco did think. Kevin kept saying it wasn't his case. He was as helpful as ever about Clyde, too.

After he left, I set out to comb the shelters again. Then I followed up one of the few phone calls that had sounded promising, but when I showed the woman a sharp nine-by-twelve color print of Clyde, she said, rather indignantly, "Why, no! That's not him."

When I got home and opened the mail, I found an invitation keyed to my state of mind. Tomorrow night, Friday, Mimi Nichols was hosting a fund-raiser for her animal rights group, which was marshaling its forces to make sure the city council passed the law regulating animal research in Cambridge.

With the invitation came some brochures and photocopies of newspaper articles about the committee. I'll spare you the details except to say that Cambridge was such a humane, progressive place that it had already banned the Draize test and the LD-50 test. Don't they sound harmless? I'd rather not talk about the Draize test. LD stands for lethal dose. LD-50 is a toxicity test in which animals—including dogs and cats—are force-fed whatever substance is being tested. The test measures the dose needed to kill half of them, fifty percent. Gee, isn't Cambridge wonderful? We were too civilized to do that anymore. And Mimi's organization was hardly pushing for radical change. The ordinance was only supposed to regulate animal research, not stop it. Research could still kill animals. It was just supposed to do it humanely. Cages were supposed to be big enough so animals could move in them. Animals undergoing painful experiments were supposed to be "monitored." What the hell does "monitored" mean? That someone gets to watch?

Even though it was a wishy-washy ordinance, I wrote out a check for as much as I could afford, filled out the little reply card to show I'd attend, put them both in the return envelope, and, stupidly, made sure that Rowdy was still safely asleep in his favorite spot in my room. Asleep. Alive. With room to move. Monitored the way dogs are supposed to be monitored, by people like me. Monitored better than Buck or I had monitored Clyde.

Clyde.

Rowdy didn't mind being awakened, and he'd never objected either to a walk or to the chance to jockey for position with other dogs, which is what he did at Mimi's by voicing his regret that Regis and Sunshine were on the other side of their wire mesh. Mimi wasn't there, but Libby was working with Zip, or at least trying. When Rowdy arrived, she had to give up.

"Could you give this to Mimi?" I asked. "It's my RSVP for the fund-raiser tomorrow."

"You coming?"

"Yes."

"Steve?"

"Not that I know of."

"That's new," she said.

102

"It's new. It's so new I don't want to talk about it. Okay?"

"Don't bite my head off."

"I didn't mean to. I'm sorry. I wanted to ask Reggie about Clyde. Is he around?"

"He took off somewhere. Did you give any more thought to the printer?"

"Is it his?"

"Sort of."

"What does that mean?"

"Ask me no questions," Libby said. "It's a good deal, right?"

"Yeah," I said. "But I'm broke. Actually, I'm saving up for a new dog."

"It's about time. No one should have to be an only dog, right?"

"Right."

We were standing by the kennels, right by the driveway, and Reggie drove the dented green Buick station wagon in so fast that I was afraid for a second he'd hit one of us, but he threw on the brakes a good two feet away.

As soon as Reggie got out of the car, before we'd even had a chance to say hello, Rowdy started to wag all over. He danced around at the end of his leash, bounced up, and hurled himself on his back at Reggie's feet. I like him to be friendly, but I didn't see the need for that ridiculous performance.

CHAPTER 15

TO MY PARENTS, TRAINING AND HANDLING CLASSES were church. I keep the faith. These days, my sabbath is Thursday evening, and my place of worship is the armory on Concord Avenue, near the Fresh Pond traffic circle, where the Cambridge Dog Training Club meets. Our sanctuary is a huge, shabby hall with a crumbling parquet floor, and the pews are rows of scarred wooden bleachers, but the place doesn't matter. Lots more than two or three of us gather together. That's what counts.

The sacred animal and I drew our lesson for that evening's service from Section 25, Sentence 1 of the American Kennel Club Obedience Regulations. Under the heading "Misbehavior," Section 25 decrees that "any uncontrolled behavior of the dog," including "running away from its handler," must be penalized according to the seriousness of the behavior. According to my interpretation of the text, bolting out of the ring wasn't as serious as biting a judge, but it was serious enough to warrant penance, fifteen minutes of heeling on leash and fifteen minutes of heeling off leash during the yelping chaos of the beginners' class. Afterward, we joined the regular class, which was no penance for my furry sinner. A dog training class meant other dogs, and where there are other dogs, there's always the possibility of excitement. For instance, a satisfying slash-and-tear could break out, and even if the joy-killing dope at the human end of the leash stops you from leaping into the thick of it, you at least get a vicarious thrill, not to mention the joy of hearing yourself praised while others are scolded.

Rowdy's hopes weren't fulfilled that night because Vince, our head trainer, nearly always prevents fights before the first snarl erupts. Besides, Rowdy knew he'd fallen from a state of grace and was determined to earn his way back. When I told him to heel, he'd bounce up, flounce around me, land in a perfectly straight sit at my left side, his front feet exactly even with my toes. Whenever I called him, he came directly to me and tossed me a smug grin. "Section 25? Me? Guilty of misbehavior?" his look said. "Must be some other dog."

"Sit your dogs," Vince ordered us.

We were lined up along one wall with our dogs sitting at heel. Those of us who show our dogs unsnapped the leashes and dropped them on the floor behind the dogs.

"Leave your dogs," Vince said, and, in unison, we all said, "Stay," put our hands, palm down, in front of the dogs' noses, and walked away. Ron Coughlin's mixed breed bitch, Vixen, was next to Rowdy, so Ron and I found ourselves together at the opposite side of the hall. In theory, you're supposed to hold still and be quiet when you leave your dog for sits and downs, but in classes, no one does. That night, we discussed Mimi's party. We don't gossip. We're just interested in people. Everyone who isn't rich is interested in people who are.

"So you going tomorrow?" Ron asked me.

"Yeah. You?"

"Wouldn't miss it," he said. "You ever been in there?"

"No. I've just been outside, in the yard. Have you been inside?"

"Yeah. How many rooms you think there are?"

"I don't know. Thirty maybe?"

"Not bad," he said. "Thirty-three, counting the

105

bathrooms."

I've always understood that you ignore the bathrooms when you count the rooms in a house, but I suppose it's different for plumbers.

"Did you count?" I asked him.

"Naw. I asked."

"Were you installing gold faucets or something?"

"Naw, nothing like that. One time was the garbage disposal and the other was a leaking vent pipe."

"Is it fabulous?"

"Not like you'd think," Ron said. "I mean, it's nice and all, but . . ."

Vince interrupted. "Handlers, return to your dogs."

During the long down, we picked up where we'd left off.

"So I expected it to be fantastic," I said.

"I've got a theory," he said. "She's too rich for that. Who does she need to impress? You know what I mean?"

"I guess so. Besides, if you've got thirty-three rooms for one person, well? What else is there to say?"

Ron corrected me. "Three people if you count the maid and what's-his-name. He's got his own place. He lives in the basement."

"Reggie."

"But it's real funny. Like, if you look close, some of what she's got is like what you'd expect, sort of. Take the kitchen. It's got four sinks, and—I see a lot of this stuff—four's a lot. Believe me."

"I believe you," I said.

"And you might not look twice at them, but they're all West German, and throw in the faucets, it's about a thousand dollars a shot just for materials. And then a lot of the other stuff she's got is, uh, ordinary. Like, the disposal I pulled out was a real piece of junk. And, you wouldn't believe, in the room where the vent pipe was she's got about, I swear, a hundred fly rods, and half of them are just cheap crap. It's funny."

"They must have been her husband's," I said. "He fished, and he tied fishing flies. Anyway, I know what you mean. The dogs are like that. Have you seen them? She's got two really beautiful pointers. One's a show dog, and the other was her husband's hunting dog. The third one is terrible looking, and it's a neurotic mess, too."

"Return to your dogs," Vince announced.

"See you tomorrow," Ron said.

By the time Rowdy had sniffed his way and lifted his leg up Concord Avenue to Appleton, it was ten-thirty. In my driveway, Shane was getting out of his car, if you can apply the word to a Mercedes. The car wash charges me truck rate for my Bronco, so maybe it isn't a car, either, but it's unquestionably a Ford, not a Mercedes. I chose it for the two dogs I had at the time, Vinnie and Danny, and I wanted room for a third dog, too, just in case. You never can tell. The point of the Bronco wasn't just room, though. It was also snow and ice. Since Danny had terrible arthritis, and Vinnie wasn't young, I wanted to make sure I had a vehicle tough enough to get through snow and ice, so they'd never have to walk for too long. (I'm talking about Cambridge—Owls Head plows its roads.) The strange thing about the Bronco, though, is that Rowdy resembles it much more than Vinnie and Danny did. People and their dogs don't necessarily look alike, but people's dogs and their cars do. Of course, a reasonable person with three Great Danes doesn't expect them to fit in a Corvette, and a person with one Yorkshire terrier doesn't need a full-size van, but there's more to it than that. How did I know to buy a Bronco before Rowdy was mine? Obviously, some force moving in Her mysterious way directed me to choose a large, powerful vehicle designed to make its way through snow and over ice. Ever since I'd had Rowdy, I'd been pleased with him, the Bronco, their resemblance, and this new instance of canine pattern and meaning in a sometimes apparently random universe.

That was before Shane and his Mercedes moved in, and before that Thursday evening, when I suddenly realized just how I looked in my kennel clothes. The jeans had originally been okay, L.L. Bean, only nineteen seventy-five postpaid, but nothing lasts forever, and they had holes in the knees. My T-shirt was new, a red one with a picture that looked like Rowdy's face and "Malamute Power," but it didn't show under the navy-blue rain poncho that had been all right ten years ago, before Vinnie—she was just a puppy—shortened the front hem and before Rowdy went after a tennis ball in my hand and slashed a hole in the poncho by mistake. And, of course, training a malamute is a workout, and the mist wasn't beautifying my hair, either.

So there we were, me with my truck, my clothes tailored by dogs, and my hair done by the Cambridge Dog Training Club, Shane stepping out of the Irish-setter Mercedes wearing one of those heavy tan English trench coats, his blond hair shining under the back door light.

"Holly. What are you doing out so late?"

"Dog training," I said. I thought of asking him in, but the lights in my kitchen are bright, and not quite all of the stains washed out of the poncho after one of my bitches, Sassy, had her puppies on it. "And you?"

108

"Working late."

"Publish or perish, huh?" In Cambridge, it's tactful to assume that people are working for tenure, not money.

"Sort of. You busy tomorrow night?"

"Yeah," I said. "I am. Another time?"

"Sure," he said. "We've got lots of time."

My machine had two messages. The first was from Steve Delaney, D.V.M. He said we had to talk.

"Sure," I said to Rowdy. "We can talk. We can have the same old conversation again. He has to do it. It's his job, right?"

I ran my hands up and down Rowdy's throat, then I sank my fingers gently into the mass of thick fur around his neck. A malamute's outer coat, the guard coat, is coarse, but if you dig your fingers in, you get to the woolly undercoat. A malamute is a sheep in wolf's clothing.

"Right?" I said. "The cats and dogs aren't his only patients, are they? He's supposed to think of the owners, too. I mean, he works for everyone, huh? And he can't keep them all himself, can he? Be reasonable, Holly. That's just not possible, is it?"

The other message was from my father. Millie was finally in labor. When I called back, he even answered the phone. Naturally, there's an extension in the barn.

"Not yet," he said, "but she's doing great. She's a trooper. You'd be proud of her."

"I already am," I said.

"We're on 'Darling Clementine,' " he said.

Bitches need very little help in whelping. Most of the time, the best thing to do is not interfere. Buck knows that, but he needs to feel that he's easing their discomfort, assuring them of his presence, and welcoming the pups into the world. The news that your father is singing "Clementine" to a whelping wolf hybrid bitch might make you think he's taken leave of his senses, but when my father becomes a musical lupine Lamaze coach, he's getting back to normal.

"I'm sorry," I said, "but I still haven't got any news about Clyde. I'm doing my best." I hated to jeopardize his new-found mental health by mentioning Clyde, but I had to do it. "It's only been four days. I'm still looking, and I've got people helping me."

"People," he said with disgust.

"What else do you want me to do? I'm doing everything I can, and there's a guy who's helping me. I've got signs everywhere. The ads are in all the papers. I've been checking all the shelters. Everyone knows he's gone. I'll hear about it the second he turns up. And I know Austin Quigley doesn't have him, because I went there. And besides, if he were that close, I'd have heard him howling. Austin does not have him."

"Someone does," Buck said. "Some bastard does."

"You could be right. I'm working on it."

"There are no single parents in a pack," Buck said. "Fatherhood lasts a good three or four years."

"I know," I said. "I've read L. David Mech and Matt Gerson, too, you know. And obviously, I've heard you talk about it. I'll find him."

"Regina's back Sunday. I'll be down then."

"Sure," I said. "Give Millie a pat for me. Sing her a verse of 'Clementine' for me."

CHAPTER 16

KEVIN DOESN'T LIKE TO BE CALLED AT THE STATION, but I had to do something. "Hey, Holly," he said. "How ya doing?"

"My father's doing better for the moment," I said, "but if I don't find Clyde, he's threatening to come down here on Sunday."

"It's my speech impediment," Kevin said. "I try to ask about you, and damned if I don't ask about your father by mistake. Let me have another go at it. What about you?"

"Aw, shucks, I didn't know you cared." Not so. When he asks how I'm doing, he means it. "Really, how I am is worried about Clyde. I don't know where to go from here except to try to find out if he's been stolen, I guess. And if he has, maybe that means I have to find out about research labs. I've been doing some reading, but . . . I don't even want to think about it."

"Yeah," he said.

"But of course, the police are assisting me in my inquiries. Right?"

Rowdy, who'd long ago discovered that I could be persuaded to pat him while I talked on the phone, lifted his head up as if I'd asked him a question. I shook my head and smiled at him.

"It's only been five days," Kevin said. "That's not long for a lost dog."

"Oh, Kevin, be serious. It's not as if he's an ordinary dog. He looks like a wolf. If he were wandering around, somebody would've noticed him, and somebody would've called me. And, believe me, the shelters all

111

know me by now. They'd call."

"I'd call you."

"You've got guys looking?"

"Yeah. What I can swing."

"What about people who steal dogs?" I was rubbing the top of Rowdy's head.

"Yeah. There's a kid down in East Cambridge I talked to, but in my opinion, he's got nothing to do with this. And I've never seen him around Fresh Pond." He didn't mean the pond itself—Fresh Pond is also what our neighborhood is called. "It was a long shot."

"Thanks for trying," I said. "What about what he does with them, the ones he steals?"

"Did I say he said that?"

"Didn't he?"

"Let's just say he convinced me he hadn't been around."

"Well, talk to him again. I will. Where does he live?"

"Not on your life," Kevin said.

"Then you do it. Find out where the dogs go. Clyde could've ended up in the same place even if this kid didn't take him. Or you know what? You can visit the research labs. How many can there be? They're not going to let just any outsider in, especially with this ordinance coming up before the city council, but you could do it."

"How is that?"

"Think of something."

"What?"

"Use your imagination."

"Sure," he said. "I'll start with Harvard. I'll tell them there's this new law that says they can't buy dogs anymore. They won't know the difference."

"Okay. Once they've got the dogs, it's all legal. I
112

know. Or maybe I *can* get in. There must be some way. I just don't know how these things work."

"Look, I probably shouldn't say this, but how long you been in Cambridge? I been here my whole life. How it works is you know somebody."

"Somebody who works in a research lab torturing dogs? Oh, sure, I know dozens of people like that. They're my best friends. We just don't discuss religion or politics. And what do I do if I find him in one of those places? He's the most gentle dog in the world. I don't think he's even brave." I hate to cry, especially over the telephone. "Kevin, do you know what they do?"

"Hey," Kevin said. "Don't think about that. If he's in one of those places, he's stolen property. I'll take care of that. I'll get him out."

"What's left of him. If anything."

You have to know somebody, Kevin had said. The members of Mimi's animal rights group were the last people in Cambridge who'd know anyone on the inside, but I called anyway and the woman who answered the phone in their office gave me the names of some of the labs and wished me luck. I had a plan. Not a great plan, but something. It involved Matt Gerson. He'd make the calls and the visits. A Harvard professor? Scientist? With a book published by Harvard University Press? He was as close to the right kind of somebody as anyone I knew. The not-so-great part of the plan was how I was going to persuade him to do it.

Faith Barlow called before I reached him.

"I'm in Belmont," she said. "And there's someone here I want you to talk to. There's a story I want you to hear."

"I can't, Faith. I'm working on finding Clyde."

113

"I know. Get over here."

Belmont is next to Cambridge, down Concord Avenue beyond Fresh Pond. The address she gave me turned out to be a yellow ranch house with an ordinary front yard and a long back lawn covered with spring bulbs. The yard ended at Spy Pond, which has water too dirty for swimming but looks pretty, anyway, especially when you sit at a table in the bay window of a little yellow house and appreciate the scene from a distance.

"So we put an ad in the paper," said the person whose story Faith wanted me to hear, a petite woman with very short, very curly dark hair who'd been a neighbor of Faith's until a couple of months earlier. Her name was Linda. "You know, 'friendly, good with kids, free to good home,' all that. And it was all true. He was friendly. And wonderful with kids. The kids loved him. I mean, they named him. His name was Grover. From Sesame Street?"

"Yeah," I said.

"The only thing was allergies. We have this pediatrician, and he was totally insistent that we had to get rid of Grover, because Jared had this sort of perpetual cold, so what could we do? I mean, we believed it was allergies. This pediatrician is really famous, and we trusted him. And now, we find out, he tells everyone that. I mean, basically, he just doesn't like dogs. He doesn't like cats, either. And I find out, he always tells people that. And he didn't do cultures or anything. He just said it was allergies."

"And somebody else found something different?"

"The allergist did! He tested for allergies, and Jared isn't allergic to dogs."

"But Grover was gone by the time you saw the allergist?"

114

"Yes. But, of course, we tried to get him back."

"And?"

"And we'd been so stupid. The guy we gave Grover to seemed so nice. Dave Johnson, he said his name was. And you could tell Grover liked him. When you give away a dog, you don't ask for references."

Oh, no? You should. I didn't say it.

"And he told us about his farm, and how Grover'd be able to run all over the place. He said his old dog had died. And he really had had a dog. That part was true. You could tell, because there was one of those wagon barriers in the back of the car. He just seemed so sincere. He seemed like a nice ordinary working guy. He was very likable. And then when we tried to call him, basically, he didn't exist."

"The phone number was for a dry cleaner," Faith said.

"I think he just made it up," Linda said. "But it was in Sudbury, which is where he said the farm was, even though there wasn't any phone listed to him there. So we didn't have an address, but he'd told us the name of the street, and we drove out there. That was three weeks ago. My husband and I went alone. We didn't take the kids. And, first of all, there weren't any farms there, just houses. And we stopped and asked about him. We were still convinced there was some mistake. But finally, we got it. Nobody there had ever heard of Dave Johnson. And then, of course, we realized it's like John Smith. There was no Dave Johnson."

"I'm sorry," I said. "My father's dog disappeared in Cambridge last Sunday night. I can't find him, either."

"We promised the kids we'd get Grover back. We shouldn't have done that."

"How were you supposed to know?"

"I wasn't," Linda said. "I do now."

115

Faith and I talked for a few minutes on the sidewalk in front of Linda's house.

"I don't know why the hell she didn't call me," Faith said. "I'd have kept him for a week or two to see if the kid really was allergic. And free to good home? Did you hear that?"

"Most people don't know any better."

"And that business about the farm?"

"Yeah. He probably tells the girls he wants to show them his etchings, too."

"They probably believe him," Faith said. Her hair looked more gray than blond, and her dimples weren't showing. "Some people will believe anything. And Linda's no fool, at least most of the time."

"Yeah," I said. "She sees it all now, doesn't she? I feel so bad for her. What kind of dog was Grover?"

"A big friendly mutt," Faith said. "Black with a big white splotch over one eye. White on the tip of the tail. You know, cute and funny-looking, like a clown. They got him at the pound. The pound. You know that's how research labs pay? They buy dogs by the pound, like they're buying meat."

"They are," I said.

"So I thought you'd want to know. I mean, obviously, this is a racket, right? It's a scam. And this is pretty close to your part of Cambridge. And they're both big dogs. I thought you should know."

"Thank you. I'm not sure if it'll help. I was sort of starting to think about something like this, anyway. I think I won't tell Buck, not yet."

"Good," she said. The dimples appeared for the first time that day. "So when do I get Rowdy again?"

"We'll do the June shows. Okay?"

"Sure," Faith said. "He's a love. He's a real honey."

Free to good home. I thought about it as I drove back along Concord Avenue toward Cambridge, past the golf course, the fast-food places, the industrial parks. How was Linda to know? What was she supposed to do? Take big, friendly Grover to the vet and have him put to sleep, put down, done in? Sell him? People who buy dogs don't want a dog like Grover. They want cute puppies, and if they pay for them, they're apt to want purebreds. So she'd tried to do the right thing, but there'd been a hitch. The world is a crueler place than she'd suspected.

Near the Fresh Pond traffic circle, I saw a black and white spotted dog following a runner on the path around the pond. In the back of the Bronco, Rowdy caught sight of him, too, and growled and yelped out a warning to get off his turf, which was, in Rowdy's view, the planet earth. I only caught a glimpse of the dog, but it was enough to see that he had some pointer somewhere in his ancestry, enough pointer to remind me of Max, and what Austin had done to Lady. I wondered if Max's days were numbered, too. But Max was worth something. Austin would know that. Somebody might even have made an offer already. Would anybody pay for euthanasia when he could get good money for the dog? Maybe yes. Maybe if he just didn't like the dog, the way Austin just hadn't liked Lady. Or, for that matter, Sissy. If he was killing off the whole family, maybe Max was next.

I was eager to get home and get hold of Matt Gerson, but I turned left onto Walden Street, pulled into a permit-only spot, leashed Rowdy, and started toward Quigley Drugs. All I'd have to do was walk Rowdy past the place, and if Max was there, he and Rowdy would both let me know.

Sissy's old car was parked in the driveway by the store, and Pete Quigley was standing at the open tailgate sorting through some cans of paint in the back. The last time I saw that car, there was a bumper sticker on the rear: "Caution. Show Dogs. Do Not Tailgate." I always notice bumper stickers like that because I don't understand why people use them. Why advertise that the dogs are valuable? It's a written invitation to steal them. Anyway, the bumper sticker was gone. I hoped Max wasn't. I was relieved to see the wagon barrier still in place inside the car, and even more relieved to see Rowdy's hackles go up and to hear Max start barking out some hearty threats.

Pete looked up from the paint cans. "Dog's locked up. It doesn't bite, anyway." He sounded disappointed, as if he were complaining about a toy that didn't work.

"I know," I said. "He's a good dog. He's just barking because he and Rowdy don't get along too well." I gestured to Rowdy. "They had a little fight once, right here." Sissy's murder somehow made me want to minimize the fight.

"It was him?"

"Yes."

"My mom told me about it." Max was still barking. Pete cupped his hands around his mouth, aimed toward the store, and shouted, "Max, shut up!"

Max continued.

"I'll go," I said. "Rowdy's what got him going. See you."

"Yeah," he said, and we headed back toward the Bronco.

I must now point out that Rowdy knew not to jump up on people. None of my dogs has ever been allowed to jump on people. Even in a little dog, it's an

118

obnoxious habit, and in an Alaskan malamute, it's intolerable. Suppose he jumped on the wrong person? A neurotic person, which is to say someone afraid of dogs, might have a heart attack. Rowdy never jumped. He arose, stood up, elevated himself to his full standing height without losing his balance or throwing his weight around. And he'd never picked the wrong person. In fact, he reserved the behavior almost exclusively for me, and occasionally for Buck, and even then, for special occasions. It was his welcome home after I'd left him alone for a long time.

So what did Rowdy think Reggie Cox had done to deserve this special greeting? Something, because that's what he got. I'm not sure whether Reggie realized he'd been singled out for an honor, but at least he didn't have a heart attack. He didn't seem to mind at all.

"What a big boy you are," he said with approval. Rowdy was still resting his forepaws on Reggie's shoulders, and Reggie was running his hands up and down Rowdy's back.

"He doesn't usually do this," I said. "Rowdy, that's enough. Get off. You haven't heard anything? About Clyde?"

Reggie shook his head.

"Rowdy, get off." I gave the leash a sharp jerk, and he finally paid attention. "We've got to get going."

Even then, with all four paws on the sidewalk, Rowdy was still playing up to Reggie, smiling up at him, tossing his white tail around.

"Nice dog you've got," Reggie said.

"Thanks," I said, rubbing Rowdy's head. "He really is a good dog. He's a honey."

I don't know why I used Faith's word. I usually say he's a sweetie.

CHAPTER 17

RON WAS RIGHT. NO GOLD FAUCETS. NOTHING GARISH, nothing opulent, nothing showy. For instance, the upstairs bedroom where one of the crimson-jacketed kids from Harvard Student Agencies told me to leave my coat had only two Matisses. Three obtrude, I always think.

My mother believed in rules, including the rules of the human social world, and she liked them spelled out in writing, which may be why I grew up thinking that Emily Post was a woman hired by the American Kennel Club to write its human obedience regulations. Consequently, just in case you were wondering, I knew better than to show up at Mimi Nichols's in my kennel clothes, not that anyone would have noticed. Or cared. After all, this is Cambridge. People here notice whether you're really asserting or merely mouthing the views expressed in the latest issue of *The New York Review of Books* and care about whether your kids go to public school because you're political or because they flunked the Shady Hill kindergarten entrance exam. Even for concerts or big parties, people wear anything from formal evening dress to embroidered Greek peasant costumes to jeans and Reeboks. Not everyone has had my advantages. I wore a silky gray pants outfit that I'd picked up at a discount in Freeport before I decided to have Faith show Rowdy in breed instead of showing him myself. As I'd suspected in the store, the outfit really brought out the shine in his coat, and vice versa. Too bad I'd had to leave him home. A stunning dog makes the best accessory.

People were pushing their way upstairs as I went

120

down, and the front entrance hall, bigger than my kitchen and study combined, was jammed with people, most of whom I didn't know. I felt awkward until I pretended that Rowdy was with me. I only imagined him—I didn't talk to him or pat him or anything—but as soon as I did that, I felt self-confident and realized the thing to do was head for the food, just as he'd have done. Ray and Lynne Metcalf had already beat me to the shrimp, which were jumbo, like giant-size Nylabones, only not ham-flavored, of course. I wondered whether my donation had been big enough and whether I could afford to give any more. That was the idea, I guess.

"Hi, Holly," Ray said. "Just arrive? Can I get you a drink?"

"Sure. What is there?"

"Red or white."

"Red."

He pushed his way through the crowd and, after Lynne and I had talked and eaten shrimp for a while, he made his way back and handed me a glass of red wine. The glass was the kind I have, but it was real, not one of those plastic things with the stems that fall off, and the wine was jug Burgundy. You don't believe me? I saw the bottles later. The white was jug Chablis. If I'd given a party like that, I wouldn't have bought good wine, either, but then I wouldn't have served shrimp or hired what must have been the entire staff of Harvard Student Agencies, which is the Cambridge solution to the problem of getting good help these days. If today's housecleaner or bartender is tomorrow's partner in Ropes and Grey or assistant professor of French at Princeton, the inherent socioeconomic inequalities of the master-servant relationship don't weigh so heavily

121

on your conscience as they might otherwise.

Once Ray and Lynne and I started talking about dogs—what else?—I forgot to imagine Rowdy, and we met lots of other people who wanted to talk about dogs, too. Lots of people? There are fifty-two million dogs in the United States, thirty-three million households with at least one dog, and eighty-eight million people in those households. See? Lots, and plenty at Mimi's party, particularly because it had a high concentration of animal lovers.

I met one exception, a fat little man. He was one of four people I met that evening who told me how much better they'd felt since they'd been on antidepressants. The first thing I asked him was if he had a dog, but he said no. Then he told me he was a psychologist and that he was doing research on thinking about morals.

"Oh," I said. "So that got you interested in the ordinance, regulating laboratories."

"Thinking about thinking about it, as it were," he said.

"What?"

"In reasoning about moral values," he said. "How does one justify one's choices? In what cognitive context does one adopt a moral stance? On what basis does one create that context?" He added knowingly, as if passing along insider information, "Because one does create it, you know."

Actually, until then, I hadn't even been sure he could put the letters *y*, *o*, and *u* together and pronounce them.

"One gives a shit," I said. Emily Post would have given me a nonqualifying score and a ladylike boot out of the ring.

After that, I was glad to run into Reggie Cox. You could count on Reggie to say "one" because he didn't

122

mean two or three. Libby was with him. They weren't wearing red jackets or carrying trays of food, and the pointers weren't anywhere in sight, so I assumed they weren't there to work.

"I'm so glad to see you," I said. "I just met the biggest jerk."

"Stick around," Reggie said.

Libby laughed. "Actually, we can't stay. I'm due back upstairs, and Reggie's got Ed's study."

I must have looked puzzled.

"We're nicer than off-duty cops," she said. "We blend better. Mimi doesn't know half these people. We're the security force. Part of it. Don't look so shocked. We know you're honest . . ."

"I'm not shocked," I said. "I just hadn't thought about it."

"See?" Libby said. "You're honest. See you later."

"Hi, Libby, Reggie," Ron said, stepping toward us, then as they walked away, "Bye." He had on a dark suit, and I could smell some powerful after-shave. "See? Mimi invites them. You see how nice she is?"

"They're here to work," I whispered to him. "They make sure no one steals anything."

"She has to worry about that, I guess. When you get called in to work here, someone's usually around. But you don't feel like they really think you're going to steal anything. Somebody's just always in and out, you know? Doesn't bother me the way it does some people. Pete didn't like it. He thought they didn't trust him."

"Pete Quigley?"

"Yeah. Sissy's kid. You know. He was here when I took care of the vent pipe."

"Oh. Doing finishes?"

"Have you had too much to drink?"

123

"No. I heard that's what he calls it. He doesn't paint. He does finishes."

"Well, he was painting when I saw him," Ron said. "And he thought they didn't trust him, because he was painting in the den where the fishing rods are, and they kept watching over him. Mimi has a thing about her husband's fishing rods." Rita once explained to me what Freud had to say about people having things about things like that. "Even though most of them are just junk, like I told you. Like that disposal."

"Maybe it was because of Sissy," I said. "That he didn't like the idea of being watched. Because she did take things. Or that's what people say."

This may be an opportune moment to point out again that just as my dogs never jump on people, Ron and I never gossip.

"Yeah? And Pete's sort of a mama's boy," Ron said. "Maybe he thought if they knew about her or something, that's why they didn't trust him. But it wasn't like they acted funny. It didn't bother me. Lots of people are worse."

"I heard what Sissy took was dog stuff," I said. "I heard she took leashes and grooming equipment. According to Libby, those shears were hers, the ones . . . you know. She says Sissy took them from her, a while ago. Apparently they were sitting there in Sissy's tack box. And you know what's weird? Libby keeps asking me when I think she can have them back. Who'd want them?"

"With somebody's blood all dripping down them?"

"Well, you could wash them. But even so."

"You know, she has fits," Ron said.

"Who?"

"Libby. Pete told me."

"Seizures? Epilepsy?"

"Yeah."

"That wouldn't make her want the scissors back. It doesn't do anything to your personality. Mostly what it does is embarrass you, if it happens in public. But how did Pete Quigley know?"

"From the drugstore," Ron said. "Libby had a fight with his mother about it, because one day Libby showed up, and his mother asked, I don't know, if she's had any fits lately or something, and someone was there. She doesn't want people to know and everything, so she told Sissy to shut up. Pete said Libby was really mad."

"How did Sissy find out?"

"Libby takes medicine for it, and she'd been buying it there."

"Oh, right. But isn't that supposed to be confidential? I mean, pharmacists don't tell people what the customers are being treated for, do they? I never thought about it. I'd hate that."

"Yeah." Ron loved the idea. "You're walking down the street and the druggist passes by and says, 'Hey, how the hemorrhoids doing? Shrunk up any lately?' Oh, boy."

"I wonder if her husband knew she did that. I have the feeling he wouldn't have liked it. Maybe that's why he killed her. I mean, if he did. He struck me as a guy who takes a lot of pride in his profession. He sort of apologized because the store was still open after what happened to her. He said people relied on him. I was surprised. I don't know why. Maybe because the place looks like such a dump from the outside."

"A far cry from this." He looked around.

"Most places are. But, you know, I see what you meant about the house. It's not that it isn't attractive. It

125

just isn't designed to impress you. I guess I would have expected silver and crystal all over the place or something."

"Yeah. If you think about it, what's there to steal?"

There weren't a lot of knickknacks. The smallest things I could see were candle holders, but there were lighted candles in them. Lifting them unobtrusively would have required some accomplished legerdemain. The downstairs bathroom had a Paul Klee drawing on the wall. Maybe the frame was bolted to the plaster. I hadn't tried to remove it.

"I don't know," I said, "but you want to know something else weird?" I told him about the printer Libby had offered me. "It seems to me that makes them strange security."

"Yeah," he said. "Reggie's kind of a strange guy, too. You know he's from Maine?"

"That doesn't make him strange. I'm from Maine, too. Maine is a perfectly ordinary place to come from. It's a good place to come from."

Ron thought that was pretty funny. "It took me a while to do the disposal, and while I was doing it, the maid told me all about him." Didn't I tell you about good help? Would a Harvard student have gossiped to the plumber? Then again, maybe the maid was one.

"What did she say?" I asked.

"Mimi inherited him. He started out as her husband's guide, fishing and hunting."

"I heard that somewhere. But is he a real guide? He has a Maine guide's license?" If so, I was impressed. That's my home-state equivalent of having a book published by Harvard University Press.

"I don't know," Ron said. "Anyway, he ended up here. You know he lives in the house? There's an

126

apartment. And he'd shovel the walks, and drive Mr. Nichols around, do odd jobs, clean up after the dogs. He shovels all the walks around here. Asked me about doing ours, at the library, and asked about keeping an eye on the place, like nights and stuff, when it's empty."

"That's a step down from being a Maine guide."

"Probably pays better," Ron said. "And he still did that, too, when the old man was alive. Drove him on fishing trips. He was the one with him when he kicked the bucket."

"I haven't forgotten about that," I said quietly. "Bee stings. My fault. Allergies. Right." I cringed at the memory.

A tall, gray-haired man standing near us turned to me and said quietly, "Forgive me. I'm intruding. You're allergic? To bee stings?"

"No. Not to anything," I said. "Especially dogs."

"Sorry," he said. "I thought I heard you mention it."

"We were talking about Mr. Nichols," Ron announced, then lowered his voice. Finally. "That's how he died."

"I know," the man said. "He was my patient. That's why I spoke up. There's a bit of a controversy about that kind of thing, you know. You see somebody walking down the street, and you can tell at a glance that he has some disease or other, do you march up to him and say, 'Hello, there. You look like someone with Addison's disease'? Or whatever it is."

"I suppose that could be a little unwelcome," I said.

"Yes, it could be. But on the other hand, what if he doesn't know? What if he's not being treated? That could be worse. And I seldom do it." He lowered his voice. "But Ed Nichols was a friend of mine."

Plumbing is a direct profession. If somebody tells

127
INDIAN PRAIRIE PUBLIC LIBRARY
401 Plainfield Road
Darien, IL 60561

Ron that a bathroom fixture has broken, he has to ask which one. It doesn't embarrass him. "What happened?" he asked.

"Ed hated the allergy," the doctor said. "Hated it. Thought it was unmanly. Denied it. I saw him a week before and wrote him a prescription for a new kit, and he paid no attention whatsoever. It was summer, June it was, and I knew he was going fishing. That's why I, uh, accost people now. If he'd had the kit with him, he'd be here right now."

"That wasn't your fault," I said.

"If I'd scared the life out of him the way I should have, he'd have had the kit," the doctor said. "Education is a medical responsibility. I've learned a hard lesson."

By that point, I'd assumed that the fund-raiser was going to be what it had been so far, a party, but Reggie, apparently on temporary leave from guard duty, started asking everyone around us to move into the living room, and I noticed Libby across the room doing the same thing.

All of us fit easily into the living room, if that's what you call a room that holds a couple of hundred people. There weren't seats for all of us, but Cambridge people don't mind sitting on the floor. Some of them do yoga. Some like to pretend they're still kids. Some think it's good for their backs. Sissy wasn't the only hypochondriac in Cambridge, which is, among other things, a city of spinal hypochondriacs, or maybe half the population has genuine back trouble from all the years of hunching over books and computers. Whatever the reason, at parties and meetings in Cambridge, you'll see a room half full of empty chairs and people all over the floor.

Mimi's dress looked fantastically expensive. All

around the neckline and down the sleeves were dozens of little pleats, and the skirt was pleated, too. It was dark green, and, as usual, I couldn't quite place the fabric. It wasn't cotton, and it sure wasn't rayon or polyester.

"Isn't she something," Ron sighed.

The speaker she introduced was a lanky blond guy in a light tan corduroy suit, but denim leaves an indelible mark. After years in jeans, you wear anything else as if it's a costume. I couldn't have been the only person there who dreaded listening to him or the only person relieved to be spared most of the details. His presentation concentrated on the aims of the organization. He talked about the Harman principles, which call for minimizing the amount of animal research, restricting it as much as possible to research on serious medical problems, and treating animals humanely. A flaming radical, huh? And, as I'd gathered from the brochures, the ordinance, while a lot better than nothing, was insipid. If the ordinance passed, institutions doing animal research would have to register with the city, but they could still do vivisection. And let's not forget that research on mascara and floor wax is, after all, research. Every year, more than fifty thousand animals are subjects in experimental research. Does that seem like a lot of animals? That's only in Cambridge.

After his talk, people asked a lot of questions, of course.

One of the questions was mine. Like Popeye, I am what I am. "How many of these animals are dogs?"

"Good question," he said. I'm sure a lot of people didn't think so. I don't want mice to suffer, either, but, to me, it's not the same. He went on. "But I can't answer it because so many labs won't release their

129

research protocols. What I can tell you, for one thing, is that fewer than five percent of the lab animals in Cambridge get any government inspection."

"So, basically, researchers can do anything they want, and they can do it in secret," someone added.

"That's what the ordinance is about," Mimi said.

His talk wasn't so bad, after all. It was all positive. Think about the Harman principles. Think about the ordinance. Think about the future. It didn't get to me until I was back home standing at the bathroom sink, removing the eyeliner that had probably been tested on rabbits and wondering how I was ever going to find Clyde. If he'd ended up in a lab, it wasn't necessarily in Cambridge. And if he *was* in a lab in Cambridge, he was one of fifty thousand or so. No, not that many. Fifty thousand a year, the guy had said. Lots of those animals were dead already.

Then I started going through the bathroom shelves throwing out anything that might have been tested on animals, which meant anything not made by Avon. I ended up with almost nothing left except a bottle of Avon Skin So Soft bath oil, which is not only ethical but effective, as any malamute handler will tell you. Diluted half and half with water and sprayed on, it gives a nice shine, and repels ticks and fleas, too.

CHAPTER 18

ONE OF MY FAVORITE BOOKS IS CALLED *HOW TO BE Your Dog's Best Friend*. It was written by the Monks of New Skete. Although I agree with most of what the monks say, there are a couple of exceptions. For instance, according to the monks, your dog should sleep in your bedroom because it's good for the dog's mental health. For Rowdy and me, it was the other way around. Rowdy would've slept anywhere. The floor by the bay window in my bedroom was his favorite spot mainly because he was used to it, and he was used to it because I sleep better when I'm breathing a dog's scent and basking in his undemanding presence. Once in a while, I'd heard Rowdy purr in his sleep almost like a gigantic house cat, but he'd never snored, and I always took off his collar so the tags wouldn't jingle.

He didn't purr or bat at me with his paws that night. It was Clyde who kept me awake, the new father of five pups, according to the message on my machine. Wolves aren't like cats. In the wild, the whole wolf pack, including the father, helps to take care of the pups. Cats. A lab at MIT was still doing a famous series of experiments on kittens and cats. The researchers sewed their eyes shut. My tax money was helping fund that. A few years earlier, my tax money—yours, too, of course—had almost paid for another great experiment. A delightful group of human beings at a place endearingly called the Wound Laboratory—it's near Washington, D.C.—had the charming idea of studying tissue damage. To do that, you need damaged tissue, right? You'd think the Department of Defense, which runs the place, would keep surplus damaged tissue lying around, but evidently not, because these bastards—pardon me, biomedical researchers—planned to get it by firing bullets into dogs and cats. Caspar Weinberger, the Secretary of Defense, stopped that experiment. That's a true story. Look it up. What *hadn't* Weinberger stopped? What had no one stopped? Where was Clyde? Sometime around three A.M., I remembered reading an article written by a doctor. It was about his medical training. He described a laboratory exercise in which he'd had to vivisect a dog that was supposed to be anesthetized, but the dog kept waking up and howling. Just reflexes, he'd been told. He'd known better. Boston has lots of medical schools. Where the hell was Clyde?

At seven, I was knocking on Marty and Matt Gerson's door. Since puppies wake up early, I'd thought that little Jason or Justin might, too, and I was right. He was sitting in a little seat that hooked onto the kitchen table, dropping what looked like Cheerios onto the floor. Marty said they weren't Cheerios at all, but some health food look-alike, and that the activity was facilitating the development of his fine-motor coordination. Rowdy cleaned up, first the floor, then the baby's face, and while we waited for Matt to finish shaving, I showed the baby how to toss the cereal into the air and let Rowdy catch it.

"It facilitates the development of eye-mouth coordination," I told Marty. It does too. Practice catching food was why Rowdy was so great with a tennis ball or a Frisbee.

Matt finally came to the table, and while he ate more of the same little O's with milk and banana slices, I filled him in on what I'd been thinking about Clyde.

"He's no place else, Matt. I've upped the reward as

much as I can. I've had signs up and ads in everywhere. At first, I thought he was just lost, too, but he isn't. And these places really do exist—right here in Cambridge."

"You're right. They do."

"And they aren't going to talk to me. I'm not going to get inside a single door."

"What makes you think they're going to welcome *me*?"

"They aren't. They aren't going to welcome anyone. But you'd at least stand a chance, wouldn't you? You've got credentials. You're a researcher."

"Not that kind. Believe me. Not that kind."

"Of course not. I wasn't suggesting you were. But that's the thing. I don't know people like that, and I don't know how else to find out what's going on in those places except to find somebody who can get in. Will you at least try calling?"

"Of course, but . . ."

"I know you don't want to. I can understand that, but I'm desperate. I wouldn't ask you otherwise. Maybe it's a stupid idea, but I don't know what else to do."

"It isn't that." He ate a spoonful of cereal. "Look, we, um, have a policy of not interfering in people's personal lives."

I interrupted him. "This isn't just personal! Don't you care about wolves?"

"Too much to keep one as a pet," Marty said.

"Would both of you be quiet and let me finish?" Matt said.

"I'm sorry," I said.

"It's okay. Look, if you need someone to make the calls, ask David Shane. Ask him to make the calls. They won't talk to me. They're more likely to talk to him. They'll return his calls."

I knew what Matt meant, of course. His own work was academic, theoretical, classy, and underpaid. Shane's wasn't. Making the calls was beneath Matt. He didn't want to dirty his theoretical hands. Let Shane do it. Really, it was good news because Shane would make the calls for me, and I didn't think he'd act like a snob about it. He'd probably even make some visits if I asked him. I knew he'd do it for me. He liked my hair. He'd said so. He liked me. He liked my father. I could get him to do it.

CHAPTER 19

KEVIN DENNEHY'S MOTHER OWNS A COMB AND BRUSH. After she's applied them to her hair, though, she pulls the whole gray mass tightly together, twists it around, ties it in a knot on the crown of her head, and gets out her principal cosmetic instrument, a hammer, and drives dozens of hairpins through the knot and into her skull. For all I know, she pounds in a few steel nails, too, or maybe the hairpins alone account for her expression, which is so pained and severe that her hair would probably stay away from her face without any hairpins or nails at all. An ex-Catholic Seventh-Day Adventist, she still worships Kevin, the last of her children left at home. She won't let him consume or even keep meat, alcohol, or caffeine in her house. They aren't good for him. She does all her housework and Saturday's cooking on Friday, and on Saturday, she goes to services, which is one reason I was surprised to find her at my back door when I returned from the Gersons' that Saturday morning. Another reason is that she knows what Kevin does at my house and yet another is that she suspects he does things there that he doesn't.

"Blessed are they that do his commandments," Mrs. Dennehy announced, "that they may have right to the tree of life, and may enter in through the gates into the city. For without are dogs."

"Revelation," I said.

It was sure what I needed. Although Mrs. Dennehy favors a fundamentalist approach to the Bible, I'd assumed that she'd worked out a quirky interpretation of most of what it says about dogs because she'd always

135

seemed to me to like them. Furthermore, although she disapproves of me, she'd also been kind to me, and everyone on the block, including the dog owners, considered her a good neighbor, not a complainer.

"My dog hasn't been out," I added. "Not out loose. And I'm taking him in right now."

"My friend Alicia just called me," she said, "and she wants Kevin to help her, and he isn't home, and he's not at the station, so I said to myself that it was my duty to help Alicia. She does not get herself worked up making something of nothing, and if she says someone has to do something, someone does."

"Oh?"

"And Alicia says the dog has been barking and whining, and usually it's a nice sort of dog. It barks, but not like this. And before the poor woman was murdered, there were two. And she doted on both of them, but now there's just this one, and Alicia doesn't know what happened to the other one, and it's not even getting enough to eat and is living in its own filth without so much as a kind word."

"That sounds terrible," I said. "What does she want Kevin to do?"

"I'm telling you, aren't I? She'd go and get the poor thing herself and bring it home, but she can't because Ralph can't abide a dog in the house, which is why Alicia doesn't have one of her own. And you won't believe it, but she likes the smell of them, especially in the rain, she says, which is funny, if you think about it, because Trapper was a nice clean dog but you'd never have known it when it turned humid. And I'd go and get it myself, but I can't with services and all, which I'm overdue for a half hour now."

"So you and Alicia want Kevin to get someone to

136

pick up the dog? Why don't you call Animal Control?"

"And have him arrested and carried off and thrown in the pound where anything could happen to him? And it could be worse than where he is now with hundreds of other dogs when Alicia says he has prizes he wins all the time, or did before, anyway."

"So Kevin's supposed to bring him back here? Just as a private citizen, so to speak."

"But he isn't here, I'm telling you, and he's not at the station, and they won't tell me where he is, so I called Alicia back, and I said to her, 'I'll get that one that lives next door to do it that's so crazy about dogs and all. When she hears she'll be glad to help, and it won't take her any time,' which it won't, either, because it's just around the corner."

"Alicia lives by Quigley Drugs?"

"The green house with the shingles and the little hedge around the front. But she won't be there now because she has to go out to the Star Market because Ralph has to have his meat loaf, and he won't eat anything that isn't perfectly fresh, so she has to do the shopping every day, which is hard on her since she started getting these headaches and won't soak her feet in water like I told her, but she does it, anyway." Mrs. Dennehy's headache remedies, by the way, work better than aspirin.

"I'll take a walk over and find out what's going on," I said. "If the dog's being neglected the way Alicia says, I'll bring him back. Okay?"

"And isn't that what you've kept me here talking about all this time? And the poor dog crying something awful, Alicia says."

I needed to talk to Shane, of course, but his Mercedes, which had been ornamenting my driveway when I'd left for Matt and Marty's, was gone. Furthermore, as Mrs.

Dennehy had pointed out, it wouldn't take me long to check on the dog. I put Rowdy in the house and, with a leash stuffed in my pocket, set out for Quigley Drugs. Although I'd forgotten the color of the house with the sprinkler in the yard, it was green, and, as I'd assumed, the barking and whining Alicia had described to Mrs. Dennehy came from Max. Quigley Drugs looked as open or closed for business as it ever had, so I risked the sign, still hanging over the door ready to concuss the customers, and walked in. I'd thought about simply marching through the gate to the backyard, leashing Max, and walking off with him, especially because I'd more or less promised Kevin to stay away from the Quigleys, father and son, but there seemed no reason to steal a dog Austin would probably be glad to have me take, or at least glad to sell. As Libby had said the night before, I am honest.

"Mr. Quigley?" I called. "Austin? Pete?"

In a little Maine seacoast town, a customer might walk into one of the gift shops to find the place empty because the proprietor was in back unpacking sachet pillows stuffed with pine needles or matching jars of real Maine blueberry honey and jam with coordinating bottles of blueberry syrup, but even in the smallest town the pharmacists know about people who find their stock sweeter than any honey, jam, or syrup. Even more than a doctor's or a dentist's office, a drugstore is vulnerable, and I'd always assumed that pharmacists took precautions, such as never leaving the door unlocked while the store was empty.

"Mr. Quigley? Austin? Pete? Is anyone here?"

But, of course, they lived in back of the place. In Cambridge, most of the mom-and-pop stores where the family lives on the premises are called spas, which means they sell groceries, cigarettes, and sandwiches, not thermal baths. Especially from the outside, Quigley Drugs looked more like one of those spas than like the good pharmacies, Skenderian Apothecary, Colonial Drug, Huron. Maybe the neighborhood customers were expected to ring a bell by the counter or even knock on the door to the family quarters?

Sissy and Austin had resisted the urge to go computer. The cash register on the counter at the back of the store was an old-fashioned mechanical model. When I checked around it, I couldn't find a bell to ring, and there was no printed sign about what to do if you needed assistance. The area to the right was screened off, probably to avoid tempting the local druggies by advertising its contents, but to the left, between a sparse display of bottled antihistamines and an even sparser one of diet aids and vitamins, was a little gate obviously intended to keep the customers on their side of the counter. I half expected Austin to pop his head out the door behind the register, wipe his breakfast eggs off his face, and order me back where I belonged, but the only sounds I heard were the banging of the little gate as it slammed itself shut, Max's muffled yelps, and my own footsteps.

By then, I should have known that no one would answer, but I needed to offer some noisy proof of my honest intentions to anyone who might walk in from the street. "Mr. Quigley? Austin? It's Holly Winter. Are you here? Are you all right?"

He answered the question the only way he could. If you're sprawled on the floor surrounded by hundreds of bottles of pills and reams of little pieces of paper torn from prescription pads, that's saying you're not quite all right, especially if you also have a wooden-handled hunting knife sticking out of your chest.

139

CHAPTER 20

EVEN WHEN HE WAS ALIVE, AUSTIN QUIGLEY wasn't magnetic, and although I'd have said offhand that anything would have warmed him up, the hunting knife hadn't. I took a couple of steps toward him for a closer look. The only medicine I know anything about is veterinary, but I knew enough to realize that he might still be alive and that, if so, nothing I could do would keep him that way. The knife had been driven into his chest right to the hilt. I'm not squeamish about blood. After all, I am a woman. I'd have grabbed the handle and pulled out the knife if I'd been sure that removing it wouldn't do any more harm.

On the wall just above his head hung a telephone, but to reach it, I'd have had to walk through the pill bottles and papers, and to use it, I'd have had to stand over him. Maybe it was a good idea not to walk there or touch the phone, anyway. My hunch that there'd be another phone in the family quarters in back turned out to be right. The room, a combination kitchen, living room, and dining room, hadn't undergone the store's recent renovation, and Pete hadn't done any finishes on its walls. The chipped enamel sink was spilling over with what must have been every dish, pot, mug, and drinking glass Austin and Pete had dirtied since Sissy died. Lined up on a grubby shelf over the sink were enough bottles, sprays, and ointments to constitute a second pharmacopoeia of over-the-counter antihistamines, decongestants, anti-itch creams, anti-allergy pills, and prescription remedies I didn't recognize. The rancid grease in a pair of iron skillets on the gas stove perfumed the place, too. The room had two windows, one on each side of the back door, but the shades were down, translucent yellowish shades that reminded me of human skin. I used my elbow to flip on a light switch by the back door, and I pulled the sleeve of my sweatshirt over my left hand before I picked up the receiver. The big black phone had buttons, not a dial. I used a grubby pencil stub I found lying on the table next to the phone to hit 911.

I stayed in the greasy little room while I listened for the sirens of the ambulance and the cruisers, but I didn't make myself at home. I didn't sit down. This may seem like a crazy thing to have done in those circumstances, but I looked at the ribbons, pictures, and trophies displayed on the wall near the table. The framed photographs included one of Lady, three of Max, four or five of other pointers, and none of Pete. The trophies sat on shelves in a crudely carpentered hanging china rack that Pete must have produced in junior high shop class. Most of the trophies had been won by two dogs with names I didn't recognize, and a few were Max's. Tucked between and in back of two medium-size trophy cups, both dusty, was a clean little silver bowl inscribed with another dog's name, Argent Silver Regis. I recognized that one. It belonged to one of Mimi Nichols's pointers, Ed Nichols's hunting dog, Regis. Furthermore, although all the other booty came from dog shows, that bowl, according to the inscription, had been won at a field trial, a competition among hunting dogs, the kind of thing Ed Nichols might have entered. Or had someone enter.

I discussed it with Rita later, and she reassured me that I was not as coldhearted as it may appear. She says I displaced my anxiety-provoking thoughts about who stabbed Austin and whether I might be next onto a

141

substitute object and that I chose something comfortably familiar but puzzling enough to focus and contain my repressed fear—namely, the question of what a bowl won by Ed Nichols's hunting dog was doing there. I focused on this distraction until the sirens interrupted my thoughts.

The first thing Kevin did was drag me out through the store, across the blacktop, and into the back seat of a black and white cruiser with blue lights on top. Kevin's name suggests his Irish ancestry. His fair complexion does, too. His face turns red when he's embarrassed and an even cuter red when he's angry.

"You had orders to stay away," he said. "Did you forget? Let me ask you something. Since your memory appears to be failing, I've got a little memory test for you. What was the first thing the officers did when they arrived?"

"They looked upstairs."

"Good. Of course, I don't know why they bothered, because you'd probably checked already."

"No. I hadn't."

"Well, well. Here's item two. What did the officers have in their hands when they proceeded up the stairs?"

"Kevin, cut it out. I know they were armed. If you call the cops because a raccoon knocks over your trash barrels, they pull their guns and go through every room in your house. That happened to Rita. She heard something one night, and you weren't home, so she called the cops."

"What made her do that?" He stretched his arms out in an exaggerated shrug, tilted his head, and expanded his chest. "Weren't you home? You could've investigated everything. Unarmed. I mean, here we have the Cambridge Police Department determining that

142

here's a situation that requires protection, but you don't need it. Not you."

"I get the point. It was careless of me."

"Careless."

"It was your mother's fault."

"My mother made you do it."

"Alicia heard the Quigleys' dog barking, and she called your mother. Your mother couldn't find you, and she had to go to services, so she asked me to check on Max. He was Sissy's dog. He's the one out back now. And I walked in and found Austin."

"And then you sat down and waited to see what would happen to you."

"Come on, Kevin. I called right away. I wasn't sure he was dead, and I wanted to get the ambulance here. And I never sat down. I stood up the whole time."

"The A Number One rule in personal safety," Kevin said. "Don't sit down."

"Well, you know what? I used the time very productively." I told him about the bowl. "So where would they have got it? One day when Ed Nichols is strolling down the street with the bowl in his pocket, Sissy sidles up to him, slips a hand in his pocket, and walks off with the bowl? Right? Come on. Or Mimi takes it to a dog show, and Sissy lifts it?"

"Why not?"

"Because, for one thing, there's no room to display stuff at shows anymore, and, for another, she's showing Sunshine, not Regis, and for another, it's a field trial trophy, and it's just not Mimi. It wasn't even hers. The dog was her husband's. He's dead, but he was the one who hunted. That's how she got into pointers. Regis was her husband's hunting dog. He isn't a show dog. You know where I think the bowl was? In her house. It was at Mimi's."

"And?"

"And Ron Coughlin was there once fixing a pipe, and guess who was painting the room where Mimi keeps her husband's collection of fishing rods? Pete Quigley. Doesn't it make sense that the dog stuff would be in the same room? Sissy wouldn't have been there, but we know Pete was."

"We do, do we?"

"Yes. And Ron said Pete was always annoyed about people checking up on him while he worked. Ron didn't mind it himself. He didn't feel as if they mistrusted him, and they didn't peer at him all the time. They just went in and out. So then we thought maybe Pete didn't like it because of Sissy, because she stole things, so he was just sensitive about it. But we were wrong."

"Wait a minute. Let me hear that again so I can get it on tape."

"Stop that, Kevin. This makes sense. Sissy used to train with us sometimes, at the Cambridge Dog Training Club, and we've never had any complaints about leashes or anything being stolen. Austin was with her there. Pete never was. The people who said she stole things were the people who knew her from shows, and Pete went to shows with her. And, look, why would Sissy ever have stolen those things? What would she have wanted with more leashes and combs?"

"What would Pete want with them?"

"Take a look at the wall in there. Ribbons, pictures, the whole display. It's all about dogs. How could he help resenting the dogs? There's not one thing about Pete, not a snapshot, not his high school diploma, not his graduation picture, not a thing."

"Like she cared more about the dogs than she did

144

about him."

"Exactly. She treated him worse than any dog, especially her own. So his mother loved the dogs, and he stole things that represented the dogs and how much she loved them. Remember, this wasn't a normal family. The dogs were Sissy's children, and the way Austin talked about Pete was nasty. But there Pete still was, living at home."

"I live at home," Kevin said.

"Your mother doesn't call you 'Baby.' "

"She'd better not."

"Sissy did. That's what she called Pete, to his face. I heard her. Maybe she did it one time too many."

"I don't know about some of this," Kevin said, "but one thing maybe I buy is that Pete's the kleptomaniac here. You think she could've been covering for him? If she knew."

"You know what makes me wonder? That bowl isn't dusty. It's the only thing in the room that isn't. I bet once she was dead, once he'd killed her, he put it out. I'll bet Mommy wouldn't let him. She wanted to protect him, and herself, too, of course. But you know what I don't get? The shears. Libby swears that Sissy stole those from her, which means that Pete did. So why did Sissy keep them in her tack box? She'd have it open at a show. Anybody could've seen the shears. If she was protecting him, why did she do that? And why did she have them there at all, for that matter? She had pointers. She'd never have had any use for those shears."

"According to Mickey, Mr. Quigley explained it. One day, his wife's looking through some book of dog stuff, getting ready to order something, and she says, 'Hey, look at this. Two hundred and something dollars for a pair of scissors.' And Pete's there, and he thinks he's

145

found a great Christmas present for her, so that's what he gets. And once he's thrown away all that dough, she has to carry them around and pretend they're just what she wanted."

"They *were* different," I said. "The other things I heard about were small. That was the only expensive thing. I guess she honestly thought he'd bought them, as a present for her. So she carried them around even though she didn't have any use for them. Until Pete found one."

"From what I heard from Mickey, this one looks like the same kind of wound," Kevin said. "We won't know for a while, but, off the top of my head, I'd say so. One blow. Real clean."

"Not quite like Lizzie Borden. Much more efficient. Where do you suppose he got a hunting knife?"

"Roach's," Kevin said. That's a store on upper Mass. Ave. "Anywhere."

"Do painters use knives? I never do when I paint. I use a putty knife, for Spackle, but that's it."

"The knife's not important," Kevin said. "Anyone can get a knife. What's important is what you said before."

"What?"

"You can grab a pair of shears, and you can buy a knife, but how do you get so efficient? That's not so easy."

CHAPTER 21

EXCEPT FOR THE TWO DAYS IN FEBRUARY WHEN I don't miss a second of the Westminster Kennel Club Dog Show, the TV I watch consists mostly of Saturday morning reruns of Sergeant Preston—Yukon King was an Alaskan malamute—and late-night screenings of *The Call of the Wild,* any version. They all make me cry. Whenever possible I don't even watch Westminster on TV. I go to New York and join the fun in Madison Square Garden. Nonetheless, as I assured Kevin, I'm not the kind of pop-culture ignoramus who would wander around the scene of a crime leaving fingerprints everywhere. Hadn't I used my elbow to flip the light switch?

"Able to leap tall buildings in a single bound," he said. "Not to mention drugstore counters. How did you manage to get into the store? And the back room? Were the doors open?"

"The doors were closed. I went through the gate to get behind the counter. I don't remember how I opened it. I didn't know he was dead then."

"Holly Winter," Kevin said, scribbling on his pad.

"I suppose I have to wait around so you can ask for my address, too. And my phone number. After all, you might have some more questions for me, and how would you know where to find me?"

"What's the number of your house again?"

"Oh, for God's sake. It's the red house on the corner of Appleton. The next one on Appleton belongs to a cop. I painted my house red to match his tape."

"You in some big hurry?"

"Yes. In case you've forgotten how I ended up here,

your mother sent me. She said it wouldn't take me a minute. She was wrong. I still have to take Max to her, and then I have a lot to do. You also seem to have forgotten about Clyde."

"I haven't forgotten about Clyde. I know this is hard for you to understand, but the world at large happens to care more about murder than dognapping. For some strange reason, there are people who consider murder a more serious crime. I can't fathom why."

"Sometimes I can't, either," I said.

Since I'd been kept outdoors or in a cruiser most of the time, it had been easy to see that no one from Animal Control or K-9 had arrived to read Max his Miranda rights and haul him away. Fortunately for him and everyone else, he'd quit barking once there were so many people around, people who had filled his water and food dishes and paid some attention to him.

What seemed like hours after I'd donated my fingerprints to the city, and been reassured that Pete would be pulled in any minute, Kevin finally told me I could go home.

"Great," I said, pulling a leash out of my pocket.

"What's that for?"

"Max. Remember? We've been over this. That's what I was doing here to begin with. Getting him for your mother. I'll just keep him until she gets home."

"No."

"She doesn't want him in the pound."

"She's never even seen the dog."

"She might have. Visiting Alicia."

"She doesn't visit Alicia. They talk on the phone. The dog is not entering my house. You weren't around when Trapper died. I'm not going through that again."

"When did it suddenly become your house? So far as

I know, it's your mother's."

"Next time you aim below the belt," he said, "how about going for my shins or maybe my knees?"

"I'm sorry. I am. Really. But, look, your mother's right. The pound is no place for Max. I'll take him home, and I'll find someplace for him. I can't keep him. He and Rowdy would kill each other. I know some people who might take him. I promise I won't leave him with your mother. Kevin, I'm really sorry I said that. It was a low blow."

"Here's what I'm going to do. I'm taking a walk down the block. When I get back, if the dog's gone, I don't know where. But I swear to God, Holly, if he's home when I get home . . ."

"He won't be. Trust me."

"When it comes to dogs?"

"Especially then."

I made three phone calls when I got home. The first was to Linda.

"I thought of something else I should've asked you," I said. "You mentioned that the car had a wagon barrier. So it was a station wagon. Right?"

"Yes. An old one."

"Do you know what kind?"

"A big American one. It was green. I'm not very good at telling what kind. Maybe it was a Chevy or an Oldsmobile. Something like that."

"Did you notice any bumper stickers or anything? I guess you probably didn't notice the license plate."

"No, sorry. Nothing like that."

"But it definitely had a wagon barrier. Sort of a metal grid?"

"Yeah, I'm sure."

"And Dave Johnson? What'd he look like?"

"Well . . . tall, I guess—but everyone seems tall to me." I remembered how small she was. "And sort of darkish."

"Eyes?"

"I don't remember. I'm sorry; I'm not very good at faces. Just an average, ordinary-looking guy, nice smile. Oh, he had on a blue work shirt, denim."

Distinctive. As long as the guy didn't change clothes more than once a month or so. I thanked Linda and hung up.

My second call was to Quigley Drugs. The cop who answered refused to get Kevin and said he'd have him call me.

My third was to Matt and Marty Gerson.

If a dog lover tells you his dog has died, but this isn't the right time to get another, it's like hearing him say he's lost his cerebral cortex, but this isn't the right time to replace it. Matt and Marty Gerson, I thought, were the kinds of people who aren't all there without a dog. Even if they didn't share my view, I was sure I could persuade them to let Max stay temporarily in their yard. Once he was there, he'd be their dog, and they'd be too loyal to part with one of their own.

Talking Matt and Marty into boarding Max was even easier than I'd expected. They spent a perfunctory five minutes supposedly talking it over with each other before they called me back, but I already knew they'd say yes. Among other things, they took pity on me because of the barking and yelping. If I'd brought Max into the house, I'd have been left with one mauled dog and no apartment. My car was a possibility, but loose in the Bronco, surrounded by Rowdy's scent, Max might have chewed or scratched a few thousand dollars of

150

damage in a couple of minutes, and I'd had enough of leaving dogs in cars, anyway. As a temporary measure, then, I'd locked Max in the fenced-in yard and left Rowdy indoors, but each dog knew where the other was and wanted at him. Rowdy, it seemed to me, had worked himself into such a frenzy that he couldn't even make up his mind which route he wanted to take to Max. First he'd try one door, then another, but he concentrated on the kitchen door that opens to the back hallway. The hallway, I should add, leads to the outside back door I share with the tenants, the staircase to their apartments, and the door to the cellar stairs. I should have known something was up. It wasn't his usual route to the yard.

To entertain me while I waited for Matt, Rowdy treated me to a concert of northern dog vocalizations. Max's repertoire was more limited than Rowdy's, but the pointer was apparently determined to compensate with volume and persistence, ceaselessly barking out a rapid-fire and increasingly fortissimo counterpoint. With double incarceration on my mind, I dragged two dog crates upstairs from the cellar. In the back hall, it became apparent that from Shane's third-floor apartment, Windy was contributing larghetto yowls to Max's staccato barks and Rowdy's allegro shifts from yip to whine to growl to roar.

The doorbell finally rang.

"Thank God you're here," I screamed at Matt. "Rowdy, shut up!"

Matt said something I couldn't hear.

"What?" I yelled.

"Do I really want this dog?" he hollered back.

"He's a wonderful dog. Wait till you see him. And just wait till you see him on point! Justin will love him."

151

"Jason," Matt roared. Or maybe it was Jonah.

Matt's arrival posed a dilemma for Rowdy. How could he keep singing out his part in the trio and still perform his see-how-cute-I-am routine for a human visitor? He compromised by directing a series of ah-woo-woo-woo greetings to Matt while edging his way toward the back door, freedom, and Max. If I'd been sensible, I'd have assembled Rowdy's crate and locked him in it, but it takes about five minutes to put the crate together and tighten all the nuts and bolts that hold the top and bottom halves together. Instead, I did something stupid. In the refrigerator was a casserole dish with some many-times-reheated Kraft macaroni and cheese encrusted on the sides and bottom. I took out the dish and put it on the kitchen floor. In the comparative silence, I could hear my ears ring.

"That'll keep him quiet for maybe five minutes," I said. "Let's get Max while he's busy. Once Max is away from here, he'll be fine. And he's so beautiful. You'll love him. I don't think we'd better try to bring him through here. Let me get the key to the back gate."

Since Rowdy and I usually use the side door of my apartment to go in and out of the yard, the gate in the fence stays locked. To keep Max secure, I'd locked it after I'd put him in. As soon as I opened it, Max quit barking, ran up to us, and sniffed my hands.

"Did you bring a leash?" I asked Matt.

He hadn't, and I hadn't remembered to take one from my kitchen door, either.

"Have you got dog food at home?"

Matt shook his head.

"Here, hold his collar and get him in the car," I told Matt. The Gersons' old gray Volvo wagon was in my driveway, a couple of feet away from us. "I'll get you a leash and some food."

"Don't bother. I can stop and get some food, or go out and get it later. I've got leashes at home."

"Okay. But let me give you some food so you don't have to stop. I've got a forty-pound bag. It'll just take a second."

By that time, Matt had Max in a sturdy-looking mesh dog crate in the back of the Volvo.

"I'll come in and get it," he said.

Windy still hadn't quit yowling, and when I finished scooping four or five cups of Eukanuba into a plastic bag, with Rowdy sniffing eagerly around, I could hear Max start up again. The intermission was over. Rowdy started woo-wooing. Then I heard banging, shuffling, and yapping in the back hall, and, seconds later, the scramble of little long-nailed dog feet on short dachshund legs running up the uncarpeted back stairs. Saturday. Rita had returned home from vacation. With Groucho.

"What the hell is going on here?" I heard Rita yell. "Holly? Groucho, get back here."

Under no circumstances does Groucho come when he's called, and although he's old enough to have more than a dusting of white on his muzzle, Rita has never once tried to teach him even rudimentary manners. I'd hardly ever heard her try to get him to do anything.

"Get back here! Quit that!" she ordered him.

"I'd better see what's going on," I said to Matt, who followed me out into the back hall and up the stairs. "Shut the doors, will you?" I added over the din.

On the second-floor landing sat Rita's suitcases and her purse. Looking up the stairwell, I saw her standing outside Shane's door. In her arms she held Groucho, who was in a state of unmistakably unaltered male

153

excitement.

"What the hell have you done?" Rita yelled at me. She is thin and petite, but one of her grandmothers was an opera singer, and Rita can belt it out like a two-hundred-pound prima donna. "Two unaltered males in the house, and I'm gone no time, and you let the third floor to someone with an unspayed bitch?"

And I'm supposed to be the dog expert, not Rita. Well, I'd asked, and he'd said Windy was spayed. I hadn't examined her for a scar. No wonder Max and Rowdy hadn't settled down. No wonder they'd rivaled so noisily. I was lucky neither of them had broken down a door to get to her.

"He told me she was spayed," I shouted. "And it's my door and my house she's tearing up. Get Groucho away from here."

"It isn't his fault."

"No," I hollered. "But it's his responsibility." That's what *she* always says.

My own apartment, as I've mentioned, is unrenovated, but not the ones I rent. Both of them have good tile bathrooms, modern kitchens, smooth walls, and expensive new doors. As Cambridge landlords go, I am exceptionally considerate. If the plumbing breaks, I try to fix it, and if I fail, I call Ron Coughlin. I return security deposits. I allow pets. Even so, my house is an investment, and, much as I love dogs, I don't enjoy the bounding, thumping, scraping, clawing cacophony of an Irish setter tearing it up. Rita carried Groucho downstairs, and as soon as I heard her door bang shut, I pulled the key ring out of my pocket and slid the master key into the lock in Shane's door. Matt followed me in.

Apart from a large puddle and a lot of red spots she'd left on the tile floor, Windy had confined her damage in the kitchen to the door, which looked as if someone had attacked it with a pair of spiked golf shoes.

"You're going to have to replace that," Matt said. He's a landlord, too.

"I'm not paying for it," I said. "You know, this is why people don't allow pets. Damn it. The next person I rent to is going to have at most one declawed cat."

Windy was frolicking around, sniffing our hands and dashing back and forth. She followed us into the living room, where I hoped to find that she'd given Shane an object lesson in having an Irish setter and a white leather couch, but I was disappointed. All she'd destroyed was what must have been a pillow. Shreds of patterned red fabric and fluffy bits of white polyester filling were scattered over the floor. As I aimlessly gathered up the shreds and fluff, Matt strolled around examining the fly rods hanging on the white wall above the couch and the mounted and framed displays of fishing flies.

"This is some collection," he said.

I remembered I'd promised Buck I'd call the insurance company. I hadn't.

"That's what my father said."

"This Payne rod's a beautiful sight. And see this reel? That's a Zwarg."

"Buck said he had good stuff. I'm taking Windy out for a second."

I ran her down the front stairs, let her relieve herself, then dashed back up.

Matt was studying the flies. "Look at these." He pointed to one of the framed displays. "See that White Wulff? And that Silver Rat? Ed Nichols tied those."

In the many hours of childhood, adolescence, and adulthood that I'd wasted listening to my father and his fishing buddies blather on, I'd involuntarily picked up a few tedious pieces of information, one of which was that my father and his friends always said the same thing I'd heard from Matt before, that they could tell who'd tied which fly.

"One more fish story," I said. "Let's get out of here."

"Sure," he said. "It would be embarrassing if . . ."

"There's nothing to be embarrassed about." I pulled the door shut, locking Windy in to do to Shane's couch what she'd done to my door and, in truth, hoping she'd wreck another door so I could present Shane with a staggering bill for damages.

"Ed Nichols was a friend of his? I never knew that," Matt said on the way downstairs.

"I don't think so. Anyway, you can't tell. He probably tied those flies himself."

"Come on," Matt said. "You're from Maine. You might as well say he left Ed Nichols's fingerprints."

"Is that true? I've never believed it."

"It's true. You can tell. If you know how. Besides, one of those rods belonged to Ed Nichols, too."

"Come on. I suppose he tied it, too."

"The tip's been mended. You can't see unless you look closely, but the mend's there. At least, Ed had one just like it. Have you talked to Shane yet?"

"I haven't had a chance. I've been busy. Remember? I don't think he's been home all day, anyway. That was half of Windy's problem, if you ask me. She needed to go out. Believe me, I'll be here waiting for him."

"When you see him, ask him where he got Ed Nichols's fishing gear."

"I have quite a few things to ask him," I said.

CHAPTER 22

"DAMN IT! THIS IS THE LAST THING I NEED."

"Holly, I'm really sorry." Matt looked sorry, too. We were standing in the hall staring at my open kitchen door, the open back door, and the darkness of early evening as if looking hard enough at the places Rowdy had been would make him materialize.

"Damn it! I should have done it myself. I should've known you couldn't hear me." What I could hear were the exhaustion and tears in my own voice.

"I couldn't, but I should've noticed. I'm so sorry."

"It's not your fault. I should've checked. Anyway, it must've been Rita who left the outside door open. She was carrying her suitcases. She probably had her hands full and couldn't pull it shut. Then she ran up after Groucho and forgot it." The stricken look on Matt's face and my own sick feeling made me add an assurance I didn't believe. "It's happened before. He'll come home."

Any dog will escape once in a while. You leave the door open for a second while you take out the garbage or bring in the newspaper, and, wham, there he goes. If he's perfectly obedience trained, you call him and he comes right back. Otherwise, you dash for the refrigerator, grab a fistful of cheese or a hunk of meat, and take off in his direction cooing, "Hey, boy, look what a treat I've got for you!" But those methods work only if he's still in hearing (and smelling) distance. Rowdy was long gone.

"I'll help you look," Matt said.

"Really, Matt, don't. He'll come home. For one thing, he knows Windy's here, and he sure knows she's in season. He'll be back in no time." My words didn't comfort me. "And Max has had a rough day. Take him home."

"Okay, but call if you need help."

"I will. I promise. And I'll talk to you soon. Have fun with Max. He needs it."

I stood by the back door watching Matt drive away and calling Rowdy. "Rowdy, come! Here, boy! This way! Rowdy, come!" I walked a little way down the block, then back home, then around the corner, but, unlike Clyde, Rowdy knew where home was, and my best bet was to be there when he arrived. If he arrived. Also, one of his tags had my phone number on it, and if the cops or a kind neighbor picked him up, I wanted to be by the phone. After all, Pete Quigley was in custody by now. Nobody'd stolen Rowdy, I kept telling myself. He'd dodge the traffic on Concord Avenue. He wasn't following the first person who patted him. I wasn't starting to cry.

I snatched the phone up the second it rang.

"Holly, where the hell have you been?" I'd always thought that Steve had the kindest voice I'd ever heard, but no one can sound kind and furious at the same time.

"Busy," I said coldly.

"I got that message. Look, we have to talk."

"We have nothing to talk about. My job is writing about dogs. Yours is killing them. I know, I know. You have to think of the owners, too. You can't keep all of them yourself. I don't want to hear it all again."

"This is crazy. I've got to see you."

"You may think it's crazy, but I don't. You're used to it. I'm not. I take it seriously. She wasn't the greatest bitch in the world, but I liked her. And you must have seen the papers. How could you consider him a

158

responsible owner? You thought he knew what he was doing? And even if you had, it just was wrong. And you want to know the latest?"

"No," he said, just the way he says it to India, his German shepherd. She listens.

"Fine," I shouted. "Don't listen. I have to get off the phone, anyway. Rowdy's gone, and I'm so worried I think I may throw up. But you know what? Austin Quigley isn't going to bring you in any more dogs to murder. Excuse me, put to sleep. Right? You don't murder them. You just put them to sleep."

"For starters, Austin Quigley didn't bring her in. His son did. Pete."

"What does it matter? She's dead just the same. What matters is who killed her." I hung up.

I forced myself to think and not to feel. This wasn't like having Clyde disappear from the van. It wasn't like giving Grover away. Pete Quigley could not have gotten him. Rowdy really had escaped before, and he really had come home soon. Logic and judgment told me to stay there. With the door to the back hall and the outside door both ajar, I sat at the kitchen table and waited for Rowdy to barge his way in, wag his whole furry eighty-five pounds around, swish his tail, give me that big, wide malamute grin, lap my face, and check out his food dish. I listened for the ring of his tags and also listened for the smooth engine of Shane's Mercedes and the sound of his well-shod feet on the wooden back steps.

So I'd been wrong about Austin, I thought. I'd assumed that whoever had killed Sissy had killed Lady, too. I'd just been wrong about who it was, Pete, not Austin, Pete, the one who'd done everything, Pete, the dog hater. If I'd returned Steve's calls, I might have known in time to save Austin. Too bad. Especially too bad for Austin, even though he'd wanted Lady dead and been glad she was. Hadn't he been wary of Pete? Hadn't he suspected? They were one another's alibi, after all. Both had said they'd been together in the men's room. Austin must have been covering up for Pete, just as Sissy had. What else had Austin Quigley known about Pete? Had Sissy been the only one who'd known that Pete was the family thief? Had Austin noticed that new bowl on the shelf? Maybe that's what had precipitated the final quarrel. Had Austin known about the stolen-dog operation too?

I went to the open back door and called, "Rowdy, come! Come on, boy! Rowdy, this way! Here!" Then I stopped. The sound of someone walking down Appleton Street turned my thoughts to Shane, but the footsteps turned out not to be his. He'd lied to me. Windy, the bitch he'd sworn was spayed, had come in season. You can't have it both ways. And even after he'd known how desperate I was to find Clyde, Shane had done nothing to help. He'd just listened. And I'd talked and talked, of course. Matt had told me to ask him about Ed Nichols's fishing gear. Well, the hand-tied flies were easy enough to explain. They'd both fished the Machias, he and Ed Nichols, both fished the Dennys, the Miramichi, too, probably. Maybe Ed Nichols had traded with Shane as he'd done with Matt. But the rods? The reels? Shane had the money to buy gear like that, but why would Ed Nichols have sold any of it? They were collector's items. He was a collector. He didn't need the money. Neither, of course, did Mimi. Could she have given them away?

Did she even know they were gone? Had she missed the silver bowl Pete had filched? What else had he taken? And Shane, with his Mercedes and his white leather, liked to impress people. If he'd had a millionaire friend like Ed Nichols, wouldn't he have name-dropped? He was just the type, and he hadn't done it. If Ed or Mimi had given him those rods and Ed's own hand-tied flies, Buck and I would both have heard. But if Pete Quigley had stolen them, Shane had almost certainly bought them from Pete. How did he know Pete?

I had a lot of questions to ask Shane, but I couldn't stand at the back door and holler his name the way I kept hollering Rowdy's, and neither the man nor the dog showed up. Besides, Shane was a liar, anyway. Reluctant as I was to tie up the phone, I decided to ask Mimi about that silver bowl and her husband's gear, and about David Shane as well. If she'd been ripped off, she had a right to know.

Mimi's recorded voice answered the phone. "No one is available to take your call right now, but if you'll leave a message, your call will be returned as soon as possible. Please wait until after the beep, which is rather loud, to leave your message." As Ron kept saying, she was a nice woman. She didn't even want her friends to be startled by the tone of her answering machine.

I left my name and number and added, "Something has come up that I think you should know about. I'm concerned about it. Could you give me a call as soon as possible? Thanks."

Not ten minutes later, the phone rang.

"Holly? This is Reggie Cox."

"Yes."

"I've got a lead on the dog. You wanna meet me? You gotta be there."

"Sure. I've got a problem here, but sure. Is this

definite? You found him?"

"You ain't gonna like it."

"Where is it?"

"Place called Bay Colony Biomedical. You got that?"

"Yeah."

According to the directions he gave me, Bay Colony Biomedical was practically down the street from my own house, in a big industrial area off Concord Avenue. Everyone knew that there were research places there, outfits that did market research and educational research, and vague things called consulting and development.

"Reggie, are you sure it's Clyde? Is he alive? Is he all right?"

"It's a wolf, all right," he said with his big, friendly laugh. "A live wolf. Live and kicking."

CHAPTER 23

I THOUGHT I HEARD IT JUST BEFORE REGGIE COX HUNG up, the sound like the whoosh of a summer wind across the Kotzebue Sound, that ridiculous, beautiful wooing, muffled and distant, familiar and absurd. Maybe he'd come home, prancing and grinning, wanderlust sated, singing his way back from somewhere down the block. For the hundredth time, I stood at the back door and bellowed, "Rowdy, come! Here, boy!" He wasn't there. Maybe I'd imagined it.

For reliable feminine protection any day of the month, I depend on a dog of either sex and any large breed—a German shepherd, a Rhodesian Ridgeback, a Doberman, a crossbreed, a mixed breed—but I prefer an Alaskan malamute. One look at a dog like Rowdy throws the average would-be attacker into toxic shock.

In Rowdy's absence, I was not myself. When I'm myself, I don't need a handgun. I don't want one, won't carry one, and don't think other people should, either. A Smith & Wesson makes a lousy pet. It's everything a good dog isn't, cold, brainless, and dangerous. Nonetheless, it was what I had left and it was better than nothing.

I pulled the case down from the back of my bedroom closet, carried it to the kitchen table, and opened it. The Ladysmith lay there, still nestled in burgundy. I suppose a revolver has one advantage over a dog. You don't have to feel guilty about waking it up. I loaded it and tucked it in my shoulder bag. That's another advantage, I guess, unless you like pocket poodles, which is what I thought the Ladysmith was, the pocket poodle of

163

revolvers.

Before I left, I ran up the back stairs and knocked on Rita's door.

"Rowdy's gone," I said as calmly as I could. "And I've got to go out. Can you listen for him?"

Her kitchen was a duplicate of Shane's, minus Windy, plus Groucho, who was scuttling around eyeing the door. To hang around home and unpack and unwind from vacation, Rita had put on pale beige pants, a white silk shirt, a thin, two-strand gold necklace, and matching earrings. Her wardrobe is the antithesis of mine. She owns dresses, skirts, good wool pants, blazers, unsnagged sweaters, and only one pair of jeans, which came from Ann Taylor and don't have holes in the knees. My jeans had a designer label, too, L. L. Bean, and no holes yet, but my blue sweatshirt with the picture of a team of sled dogs was the same one I'd been wearing when I'd set out for the Gersons' that morning and had spilled coffee and dog food on since, and I wasn't wearing any jewelry, unless you count the revolver.

"I'll leave the back window open so I can hear him," Rita said. "Do you want to borrow something to wear?"

"I'm wearing something already."

"I couldn't help noticing. Why do you do this to yourself? You have other clothes. Where are you going?"

"Hostile," I said. "That's what you'd say if I said something like that. Just listen for Rowdy, will you? And let him in if he shows up. You've got my key?"

"Yes. I'll leave the window open. Stop in when you get home, if it's not too late."

"I will. Listen for him. Call him."

Once I was outside I decided not to walk. Even with

164

my fashionable little handgun, I was feeling nervous. I wanted to get there as quickly as I could. Besides, I didn't know what kind of shape Clyde was in. I might need the Bronco as an ambulance. Or a hearse. "Live and kicking," Reggie had said. But he'd laughed, too.

Bay Colony Biomedical was hard to find. It was at the far end of one of those narrow lanes that run off Concord Avenue beyond the Fresh Pond traffic circle, one of the ones that start out as ordinary streets and degenerate into rough once-paved driveways and alleys running between, around, and beyond warehouses and barren industrial buildings and ending near the railroad tracks. It was an area I'd never liked, an area that smelled and felt dirtier than it looked in the Bronco's headlights, as if some ancient, invisible pollutant rose from it. My eyes scanned every dark corner for Rowdy. He could have run this far. He could have gone anywhere.

I missed Bay Colony twice because the lettering on the sign was small and the building somehow not what I expected. I was expecting some dark Transylvanian tower surrounded by lustrous, evil mist, I suppose, or else a minimalist, windowless white concrete edifice mounting story after story beyond high rolls of barbed wire. From the outside, it could have been any ordinary lights-out weekend office building, the local headquarters of a chain of discount clothing stores, the distribution center for a new line of educational toys. A little spotlight illuminated the sign, which hung from a white post with daffodils in bloom at its base. Reggie Cox wasn't kneeling there sniffing the flowers.

The building had a parking lot at one side. I pulled the Bronco in and left it there, right next to the only other car in the lot. The other car was a red Mercedes.

165

Reggie wasn't leaning on the Mercedes or running his hands over its chrome. When I got out of the Bronco, he didn't materialize from the shadows. Neither did Clyde.

Showing dogs will teach you to hold your head up and stride briskly along even when your knees are knocking together faster than your heart is thumping. I walked through the parking lot, across a squishy-feeling lawn, and straight to the front door. Did I expect to find a doorbell, ring it, and have Reggie greet me and offer me a drink? The doorway was dark, the door locked. I didn't knock.

I squished back across the lawn, crossed the parking lot, passed both cars, and made my way to the rear of the building, where I found what I was looking for, another door, hardly visible in the darkness. I ran my hands over it searching for the knob. The door felt like metal, a heavy fire door with peeling paint that flaked on my hands. The big sphere of a knob turned easily in my hand, but I had to shove hard on the door before it budged and swung in.

Kevin Dennehy has more than once called me naive. He must be right. After all I'd read and heard, I still hadn't freed myself from the mental link between dogs and barking. If there are dogs here, I thought, why can't I hear them? Are all the doors those same heavy, soundproof metal ones? Do they muffle the barks and yelps? And where the hell was Reggie Cox? Hadn't he intended to meet me? Had he left me on my own? I wanted to call Rowdy. I wanted to shout out his name.

The corridor that stretched in front of me, overilluminated by fluorescent tubes hanging from acoustic tile, could have been an elementary school hallway stripped of its lockers. The first few doors I came to weren't metal, but ordinary varnished wood, with little rectangular windows above the knobs. I peered in, but the lights were out in the rooms, and I couldn't see a thing. Offices, I guessed.

The next door was different, sturdier looking than an office door, and not varnished but, like the corridor walls, painted that eggshell tan that isn't supposed to show dirt and does, anyway. It was a swinging door with a stainless-steel plate, the kind that's supposed to keep dirty finger marks off the eggshell paint that isn't supposed to show them. I put my hand on the cold metal, took a deep breath, and pushed. The door moved inward.

The room reminded me of my junior high science lab, but it was narrower because of the mesh cages that lined the two long walls and the wall at the far end of the room. Down the center ran a stainless-steel table, something like a vet's exam table but longer. More overhead fluorescents washed the color out of everything, even the caged dogs voicelessly trying their barkless best to greet me or maybe even to signal my presence. One large dog in a small cage at the far end of the room retained his voice. The sight of him gave me courage. The sight of my own dog always does.

The wall to my left, the one with no cages, had glass-fronted cabinets on top, and underneath them stretched a long countertop, a work area with a row of metal stools. On the stool at the far end of the counter, next to another swinging door, sat David Shane. His lab coat was as white and starched as Austin Quigley's had been until that same morning.

"I didn't know you wore glasses, Shane," I said. They were horn-rims, the only unflattering thing I'd ever seen on him. "But, then, there's quite a lot I didn't know about you, isn't there? Why didn't you tell me you had so many dogs? I thought you had only one, and I thought she was spayed."

"She is." That flashy smile must have worked for him so many times that he'd never realized its power to work against him.

"I guess you don't know her very well," I said. "She's in season."

He looked straight at me, as if good, wholesome eye contact could keep my gaze fixed on his and away from the dogs. There were twelve cages in all, twelve dogs.

"You don't know me too well, either, do you?" I said.

"Well enough." By then, he must have caught on that the smile wasn't functioning up to par, but he couldn't stop it.

"I may look like your same old landlady, but I've undergone a sea change, you could say. Hackneyed but true. Only I haven't been washed in water. I've been washed in blood, and I've been reborn."

He must have thought I was joking—or losing my mind. He laughed.

"As a sort of new Abe Lincoln," I said. "Defender of the Union. But I'm one up on Abe. I'm the first president. The first president of the United States of Dogdom. And a woman at that. Imagine. But that's beside the point. The point is emancipation. Get it?"

"I bought every dog here," he said. "There are two sides to this, you know."

"Sure. The wrong side and the dogs' side," I said.

"Cut the crap. Rowdy got here by mistake. Take him."

My father's timid, wary gentleman wolf stood wide-eyed in a cage next to Rowdy's at the far end of the lab. Clyde's cage, like all the others, was just large enough to hold him and just too small to give him an inch of

168

space to move.

"Did Clyde get here by mistake, too?" I asked. "He looked like every other dog? It was an accident? He didn't even remind you of a wolf? Or you needed a wolf so you could test mascara or develop a better fabric softener, right? Can't be done without a wolf. So when you saw him in my father's van, you mistook him for a stray and decided to contribute him to research? What the hell do you do in this lab, anyway?"

"How did you get in here?" The smile had finally disappeared.

"Remember? I've undergone a mystical transformation. I passed right through the walls. And you haven't answered my questions."

"I did not take your father's dog. I'd never have done that, Holly. Someone else was here when he came in. I wasn't here."

"Does it matter? You knew who he was. Tell me something. I'm curious. He's a big dog. How much did you pay for him? You bought him by the pound, didn't you? How much was he worth to you per pound? And how much is left of him?"

"This is a prep area," he said, as if I'd asked for a guided tour.

"How nice for you," I said. "Because I'm about to take a close look at Clyde. And when I'm done, I'm going to do to you exactly what you've done to him. If he's been neutered, Cambridge is going to be filled with a lot of wailing women, pretty boy."

"This joke has gone far enough," he said. "Take your dog. Take the wolf. And get out. I won't press charges."

"I will," I said.

"You don't seem to understand. I bought these animals."

"They aren't animals," I said. "They're dogs."

He couldn't seem to understand that I wasn't kidding.

"You're making a fool of yourself," he said. "I paid for every one. Researchers have to. There's no law against it."

"You seem to have forgotten what I just told you. I'm the new commander in chief here. Actually, I'm the new head researcher. And for my experiment, I need a subject. A healthy, talkative male. And all I've got so far is a recalcitrant one. I've asked you a whole lot of questions, and you haven't answered one."

I reached into my shoulder bag and pulled out the Ladysmith.

"You're in big trouble," he said, his deep voice sounding a little more high-pitched than usual. "You don't like it, but buying these dogs was not illegal. I didn't steal them."

"So Pete Quigley did," I said. "Some of them. Big deal. You were his market. But tell me something. Where did you get my dog? Where did Rowdy come from? Did Pete bring him in, too? Tonight? I thought Pete was locked up by now."

Shane reached up and took off the horn-rims. His hands were shaking.

"You're making a mistake," he said. He stood up suddenly. The metal stool toppled over with a clang. He jumped.

"Speak, boy," I said. "Talk to me."

"You're off base. Where'd you get that name? Wait a minute. That was that woman who was murdered, right? Quigley? From the drugstore?"

"Good boy. Pete is her son. He's a sick character. Almost as sick as you. Keep talking."

The dogs knew something was going on. A beagle

was trying to raise his head and bay, but his cage didn't give him much headroom, and when he opened his mouth, no sound emerged. The Akita hurling himself against his wire mesh door got to me, too. He was a giant, handsome dog who'd once had a giant, handsome voice to match his looks.

"I swear to God I've never heard of him," Shane said. "This is crazy. I buy animals. I'm entitled to. But not from this guy. I've never heard of him."

With the revolver still in my right hand, I stuck my left hand back into my shoulder bag, pulled out a leash, and backed step by step toward Rowdy's cage at the far end of the lab.

"You are very slow, Shane, and I am very angry. This is no joke. First, you answer every question I've asked you. Lightning fast. Then you help me get every one of these dogs out of here—Rowdy and Clyde and every other dog—or, I promise you, I am going to debark you, and the only anesthetic you'll get is the same one you gave to these dogs. None."

"That's not true," he protested. "For God's sake, stop this. It's crazy. I'm talking now. I don't ask where the dogs come from. They get brought here. Usually at night. It's all private."

I took my eyes off him for a second to scan the latch on Rowdy's cage. Just as I was about to release Rowdy, I heard the swinging door, the one next to Shane, not the door I'd come in. Through it stepped Reggie Cox. I dropped the revolver in my bag.

I'd threatened Shane. Reggie Cox gave him no more warning than any other Maine guide would have given his animal prey. Shane's wrestling coach at Andover or Exeter or wherever wouldn't have been proud of him. He didn't put up any kind of a fight. He never had a chance. In a couple of seconds, it seemed, Reggie had him as securely trussed in clothesline as if he'd been a dead deer strapped to the hood of a pickup truck. With a wide strip of silver duct tape across his mouth, Shane made no more noises than his debarked dogs, but I guess Cambridge had taught him that expressing his feelings was good for his mental health. He wet his pants.

I opened Rowdy's cage, fastened his leash to his collar, and let him out.

CHAPTER 24

"THOUGHT FOR A SECOND THERE YOU WERE GOING TO save me trouble," Reggie said jovially.

My thoughts came in slow motion, frame by frame. Pete Quigley, a thief, but a petty thief, a city kid who wouldn't know a fly rod from a curtain rod. Kevin asking the right question: "How did he get so efficient?" I knew the answer, and it wasn't by spackling walls with a putty knife. How? By skinning and butchering deer. Moose. Bear. The printer Libby had offered me. Something Ron had said. He shoveled driveways, looked after people's houses. He'd looked after them, all right. The dog show. Pete, Austin, Sissy. Mimi and her retainers, Libby and Reggie. With the gracious social reflexes of a princess and the egalitarian spirit of a Cambridge liberal, Mimi had smoothed over some awkwardness. She'd introduced everyone to everyone else, not omitting the Maine guide who shoveled the walks, hosed out the dog pens, the capable guy who did everything for Mimi, people said, her diamond in the rough. Had he done it for her? I couldn't imagine why. And that sweet way with dogs, maybe something about his scent, the rumble of his voice. He almost hadn't needed to steal them. He must have just appeared, and they'd trailed after him like rats after the Pied Piper. Lab rats. The connection to David Shane, who hadn't lied, who'd bought those dogs from Reggie, the dogs and the fly rods and Ed Nichols's hand-tied flies. Shane probably hadn't even known where they'd come from. He'd been offered them just as I'd been offered that printer. "Don't ask," Libby had said. Shane probably

173

hadn't. But he hadn't needed to ask about Clyde or Rowdy. He'd known their names. He'd bought them anyway.

I thought I knew everything. Except why. And whether he knew I knew. Shane hadn't spoken Reggie's name. If he didn't know, why tell him? Play innocent. Take my dogs, get out, and worry about the others later.

He was still standing near where he'd dumped Shane.

"Maybe you just didn't wait long enough," I said.

He gave that same laugh. "What were you gonna do? Turn one of your wolves loose on him?" Good. He'd been listening from behind the door, not watching, and I'd tucked the little revolver into my bag before he'd seen it. He'd been otherwise occupied.

"I'd have thought of something," I said. "That son of a bitch stole my dog."

"Your big, ferocious dog, huh? He's a real tough guy. Both of you are pretty tough, huh? You and all the rest of them bastards around here, thinking you're tough, thinking you're so smart."

"If I were so smart, I wouldn't be here now."

"I know who you are," he said. "People talk about you. Holly Winter. Libby told me all about you. Showed me your name in one of them dog magazines. Sneaking around, dropping hints like I don't know nothing. I'm onto you, see? You drop this little hint, say any damn thing you want, and it goes right over my head, right? Say anything to that dumb jackass, and he don't get a thing, right? Call the dog honey, right? Honey. Just happen to be nosing around the drugstore, right? And you give one of them innocent looks. And I'm such a dumb jackass, I don't get nothing."

A honey, I'd called Rowdy. I remembered saying it because it wasn't a word I usually used. I'd heard Faith use it, and I'd said it. Otherwise, I still didn't know what he was talking about.

"Drop the act," he said.

"I'm not acting. All I want is to take my dogs and go home. This whole thing can end there."

He pitched his voice high. "Oh, Reggie, help me find my poor lost wolf." His voice dropped again. "Bitch! Hanging around pumping Libby. But she didn't tell you nothing, did she? Did you ask her how good in the sack I am? Did she tell you?"

"She's crazy about you, Reggie."

"Damn straight she is. The old lady kicks her around, too. Worse than the old man did me. You should've seen him. You know I watched? You know that? I watched. He knew, all right. He knew."

"Ed Nichols?"

"Shut up, bitch! I'm so dumb I'm invisible, right? I'm standing there, six feet of me, and you and all your rich friends are talking bee sting kits, and I'm deaf and dumb, right? Jesus Christ Almighty, I'm so deaf and dumb, I'm not there."

I started to say something.

"Shut up! You know what started this? Another loud-mouthed bitch, that loudmouthed bitch and her stupid allergies. Can't just hand over the prescription, right? 'Oh, gee, so you're allergic, too? Isn't that interesting,' she says, and then I can see by that look on her face, she's spotted me, and she's gonna run through it again, and there's old Mimi standing there ready for an earful."

He'd not only misinterpreted everything I'd done, but overestimated me as well. I'd had all the pieces, but I'd acquired them accidentally, and I hadn't put them together. The guilt-ridden doctor had done his best. He'd given Ed Nichols a new prescription for a beesting

175

kit. He'd warned him. And I'd known that Reggie was the one who did everything. He drove the car, shoveled walks, ran errands, took Ed fishing. Ed and Mimi Nichols didn't run their own errands. They had them run—by Reggie. Let Reggie take the prescription to the drugstore. Let him carry the bee sting kit. If anything happens, Reggie will know what to do. He's so capable. Reggie can do anything. He'd sure known what to do.

"You filled the prescription at Quigley's," I said. "And at the show, Sissy remembered? But if you forgot the kit or if he forgot it, nobody would have blamed you."

"Damn straight. Nobody did." The laugh was louder than ever. "Then that little bitch opens her mouth, and I hear what's coming sooner or later. Old Mimi'd be saying, 'Oh, no, Ed's bee sting kit was right in his closet where he left it,' and she's gonna chime in with, 'Oh, but this man here had his own kit.'"

"On the trip when Ed died, in June," I said.

Have you ever had real Maine blueberry honey? June is when the bushes are in bloom. That's when the bees are turned loose, thousands of bees.

"In Cherryfield?" I asked.

"Deblois."

Deblois is next to Cherryfield, not far from Machias, where Reggie had grown up. Deblois consists almost exclusively of blueberry barrens. They stretch for mile after mile. The signs warn you to stay away when the bees are loose. Even if you're not allergic, it's no place to wander around.

"Didn't he see the signs?" I asked.

"Not the way I took him," Reggie said. "You thought I was so dumb, just like Nichols did. Big man, mighty hunter with his picture in the paper."

"You caught his fish," I said. "You probably shot his deer, too." Guides will do that, or all but. The guide hooks the fish, plays it, and when it's practically out of the water, the guy who's hired him—the sport, people say in Maine—takes the rod. Some sports don't even bother to do that. "Is that what burned you? You got tired of being kicked around? So you took him to where the bees were? And you carried his kit, right? You probably carried everything. All his gear. So when he got stung, you had the kit."

"You know how much that tight bastard paid me?"

"Not enough," I said. I had Rowdy hauled in close to me, but I believe that if I'd let him go, he'd have run up to Reggie, raised himself up, and licked Reggie's face.

Reggie was ignoring him. He was busy talking about himself. "I'm here two weeks, and I'm keeping my ears open, and I get it all, see? I'm migrant labor, see? He's a cheap bastard, and I'm too dumb to work it out."

"You got away with it. Nobody ever suspected anything. And you know what? Nobody thinks you had anything to do with the Quigleys. Because you're right. About being invisible?"

"Damn straight," he said.

"And you'll get out of it fine," I said. "Honest to God, it may have seemed as if I was checking on you, but all I ever wanted was to get the dog back. And Shane will keep his mouth shut. You think he wants people to know what he does? He never told me. He's ashamed of it."

"He's already a dead man."

"He won't talk, I'm sure of it. You don't have to kill him."

Until then, we'd stayed at opposite ends of the lab. Reggie was still standing by the swinging door, right next to Shane, and I was leaning against the cage that had been Rowdy's. Reggie laughed again and kicked Shane as if he were kicking one of the tires on a used pickup he didn't intend to buy. Then he marched suddenly toward me, past the silent cages and the long steel table, and grabbed Rowdy's leash from my hand.

I'd wondered whether he had a knife. Now I knew. I hadn't even seen him pull it. It was another hunting knife. I'd only seen the hilt of the one he'd used on Austin Quigley. This time, Reggie's hand covered the hilt, and I could see the blade. The shiny metal glittered as he held the cutting edge to Rowdy's throat.

CHAPTER 25

MANY ESTEEMED EXPERTS ON DOG TRAINING BELIEVE that dogs are natural mind readers. Stay, Rowdy, I thought loudly. Good boy. Don't move.

"Dumb dog," Reggie said. He had the leash hauled in tightly, and Rowdy was as immobile as if he'd been stacked up for a Novice stand-for-examination exercise. Was he reading Reggie's mind? I doubted it. "Do anything for your damned dog," Reggie added, "you and all the rest of them rich bastards."

"That's right," I said. "So what do you want me to do?"

Rowdy looked completely calm, patient, almost bored, as if he were waiting out some unaccountable delay in judging. In the cage beyond him, the Akita looked anything but bored. "Aggressive toward other dogs" is what the books say about Akitas. Reggie probably hadn't read the books. His back was toward the cage, anyway.

"Libby told me when that rich old bastard Stanton got his, you wrote some story about it. And they paid you for it, too."

"Not very much," I said. Rowdy, stay.

"You write about dogs?" he said. "That's what you do?"

"I realize it strikes some people as a frivolous way to make a living," I said, "but it's honest work."

"A lady writer." He sneered.

"Did I ask for career counseling?"

"Smart-mouth bitch."

His sudden movement startled me. With the knife still

179

poised at Rowdy's throat, Reggie yanked on the leash and dragged Rowdy toward the counter where Shane had been seated. The long steel table blocked my view of Rowdy, but he must have had to step on Shane. Reggie grabbed a pad of yellow legal-size paper that was lying on the counter and slid it down the steel table toward me.

"Write," he said. "Write to your boyfriend."

"What?"

"The cop. And don't try and get funny."

"What am I supposed to say?" I took a couple of steps toward the steel table.

"You're gonna confess. Your crazy father carves up old wrinkle face, and you take care of the husband yourself." He gave Shane a kick. "And pretty boy here."

"Nobody's going to believe that. Why would I have killed Austin Quigley?"

"You're the writer." Reggie was enjoying himself. He gave me that big smile. Then he dropped the leash, grabbed Rowdy's collar, pulled hard on it, and, with his other hand, lifted the knife up to the light and tilted the blade back and forth.

"Austin knew my father did it," I said quickly. "He saw him, and he was threatening to tell the police. Unless something. Unless he was paid. His business is failing. The shelves are half empty, and he just did some renovation. It must have cost something. He needed the money, and he hated his wife, anyway. He was glad to be rid of her. But I couldn't pay him because I'm only a dog writer. I didn't have the money. So I found a better way to shut him up. Will that do?"

"Nice," he said, but the knife was back at Rowdy's throat. "And Robert Redford here stole your dog."

"He does look like Robert Redford, doesn't he?

Someone else said the same thing about him." I took another step toward the table and toward the Akita. Just one more step would put me closer to that cage than Reggie was, if Reggie didn't move. In dogs we trust. "But he did buy the dogs," I added. "I could kill him for that. That's credible. Maybe you have a future in dog writing. You could take over for me at *Dog's Life*. I've already started the next column for you. It's about submissive urination." I took that next step toward the table. "How did I kill Shane? Did I stab him, too? You know what? I just had a great idea. Why make it up? Let me do him in. Then I won't have to invent it."

The man had deliberately led Ed Nichols to his death, withheld the bee sting kit, and watched the poor guy die. He'd stabbed Sissy, he'd stabbed Austin, he'd been an accessory in murdering God knows how many dogs, and now he intended to kill both Shane and me, yet I swear that he looked shocked when I proposed doing no more than giving Shane what he deserved.

"Let me get this down on paper first," I said. "Toss me a pen, will you? There must be one on that counter. Never mind. I've got one here."

The Akita was risky. As I'd hoped, Reggie glanced first toward the counter, then toward me. I'd undone the clasp on my shoulder bag. "Put your hands on the table," he said.

"No, really, I've got a pen right here," I said.

Cramped though he was behind the wire mesh, the Akita started lunging and hurling himself at his door.

"Watch out!" I yelled. "His door's opening!"

Reggie turned his head. I took one more step toward the Akita, reached into my bag, pulled out the Ladysmith, and aimed it at Reggie.

"Gee, it isn't a pen, after all," I said. "It's something

181

even mightier."

And my beautiful dog? He trusted me, even as he must have felt that blade start to press hard on the soft fur of his throat.

"If you so much as splice one hair on his coat, I will shoot you," I said. "Don't even think about it. Get that knife away from him this second."

Reggie held completely still, as if he hoped first to stop time, then to reverse it.

"This really is happening to you," I said. "It's not a dog story. If you hurt my dog, I will kill you. Move that knife very slowly away from his throat. Very, very slowly. Now."

Reggie's eyes shifted back and forth, toward me, toward the Akita, toward the knife, but he moved the blade a couple of inches away from Rowdy.

"If I even start to wonder whether you might throw that knife," I said, "I will shoot you. Your hand will move very slowly. If it even starts to move quickly, I'll shoot. In case you wondered, I am a good shot. Remember? I come from Maine. When little girls in all the other states were dressing their Barbie dolls, I was out back with my twenty-two. I don't remember learning to shoot any better than I remember learning to walk. I always knew how. Get it?"

"Yeah," he said.

"Then move. Hold the knife by the blade, put it gently on the table, turn the hilt toward me, and give it a gentle, gentle push in my direction. Now."

He did as he was told, but we weren't out of danger, of course. Reggie still held Rowdy's collar, and my beautiful, trusting dog still stood right next to him. I could force Reggie to let go of the collar, but what would Rowdy do? Would he come instantly when I

182

called him? Or would he ignore me, rise up in the air, and put his paws on Reggie's shoulders? If so, or even if he lingered long enough for Reggie to get hold of him, his huge body would completely shield Reggie. Did Reggie believe I'd shoot through my dog? I'd risked Rowdy's life already. The bluff had worked then, but I thought Reggie must have seen through it by now. Once he had the chance, I thought, Reggie would turn my dog into a massive, living buffer against the little .38 revolver.

Rowdy and I had spent hundreds of hours working on his recall. If he did what he'd been trained to do, he'd dash toward me the second he heard that command. He'd ignore anything Reggie did or said. He'd ignore the Akita and all the other dogs. If. I remembered him off leash at the show, dashing around in circles, entertaining the officials and the spectators, vaulting out of the ring. When he'd put on that performance, he'd known he was at a show. And now? Just how accurately had he assessed this situation? Would he come straight to me? Or would he let himself become the hostage I could never sacrifice?

He was the least obedient and most intelligent dog I'd ever owned. I gambled that for once, his intelligence would tell him to obey.

"Good so far," I said to Reggie. "Just keep it up. Hold your right hand high up above your head."

He did.

"Fine," I said. "Now, with your left hand, undo Rowdy's leash. Let him loose." Instantly, I called, "Rowdy, come!"

As I'd expected, Reggie started to crouch and reached out for a fistful of fur or the tip of Rowdy's plumy white tail, but he was too slow. Rowdy galloped toward me, veered around the end of the metal table, and planted himself squarely in front of me, close enough so I could have patted his head, but not between my feet. It was a perfect recall. In the ring, with an American Kennel Club judge scoring him, it would have earned us thirty points. In that lab, with Reggie Cox reaching for his tail and trying to take refuge behind him, it probably earned us our lives.

And people say obedience training ruins a dog's personality.

"Rowdy, heel," I said. "Good boy."

CHAPTER 26

ALWAYS CARRY AN EXTRA LEASH. YOU NEVER CAN tell when you'll need it. Mine was in my shoulder bag. I dropped in the knife and took out the leash. I fastened one end to Rowdy's collar and held the other end in my left hand, just as most experienced handlers do. It makes sense. The dog heels and sits at your left side. If the leash is in your left hand, your right hand is free to open doors, carry shopping bags, or grasp the pearly little revolver that was your father's idea of the perfect hostess gift.

In back of me, the door of the cage that had held Rowdy stood open. From the cage next to it, my father's terrified wolf dog stared at me. With the revolver trained on Reggie and with Rowdy at heel, I edged away from Clyde and the empty cage.

"Guess what?" I said to Reggie. "There's an unexpected vacancy at this establishment. We just need to ask one guest to change rooms. He won't object. See that golden retriever? The one in the last cage, right by that noble scientist, David Shane. When I tell you, not before, you're going to lower your left hand, open that cage, then get your hand back in the air. If you move too fast, or if you hesitate, or if you say one word, or if you do one other little thing I don't like, I'll shoot you. Do it now."

As I'd instructed him, he reached toward the cage, undid the latch, and opened the door. I had no idea what Shane had done to the dog besides removing his vocal cords. I wasn't even positive the poor golden would be able to walk after who knew how long in that cage. But

185

he was a golden. He'd try. They always do.

I smacked my lips together, whistled, and called him to me. "Come here, boy! That's a good dog. Come!"

He walked stiffly, but he wagged his tail, and, of course, he came to me. Golden retrievers are the best obedience dogs on earth. I was betting that if this one had had even one or two lessons, he'd come when he was called. Besides, goldens know I'm one of their own. That's why I'd picked his cage. I hated to jail him again so soon, but I had to—Rowdy hates competition—and the golden didn't seem to mind. Besides, Rowdy's vacant cage was larger than the one the golden had just vacated.

"Your turn, Reggie," I said. "Your room is ready. Climb in. Feet first. Oh, is it too small? Well, you're in good company. All the other guests here have cramped quarters, too, and I don't hear them complaining. Now, why is that? Pull the door shut."

The metal clanged. Now I had them in one place, Reggie in the cage, Shane on the floor nearby. Rowdy and I moved right near them. With the little revolver trained on Reggie, I slipped the loop of Rowdy's leash onto my wrist, then used my left hand to rip the duct tape off Shane's mouth.

"I hope you didn't plan to grow a moustache soon," I said. His pants were still wet. I was almost starting to feel sorry for him. "Having trouble talking? Cat got your tongue? Do you have cats here, too? Let me take a look around." I didn't want to see any more, but I had to know. I stepped over him and pushed in the swinging door through which Reggie had appeared, the door next to his new cage. I leaned against the open door and kept the Ladysmith trained on him. I looked in. The inner room held no cats, no rabbits, no mice, no rats. All of

186

the creatures in there had once been dogs. The lab where we'd been, the first room, the outer one, was just prep, Shane had said. He hadn't lied.

I moved back toward him and let the door swing shut. I never wanted to open it again. I didn't feel sorry for Shane anymore.

The Akita was stirring again, still trying to bark, still making a grotesque joke of himself every time he opened and closed his jaws, bared his teeth, and made not a sound. The golden had been some family's pet, I was sure. The beagle, too, I guessed, and probably most of the others: the handsome shepherd-collie mix with the thick ruff around his neck, the two medium-size brown dogs, the big black dog in the cage next to Reggie. I didn't know their families, of course. The only one whose family I thought I knew was the one I'd seen spread out on the table in the inner room, the big black mutt with the splotch of white over one eye and another splotch of white on his tail. I was pretty sure his name was Grover and that he'd been good with kids.

I'll tell you about only one other thing I saw in that inner room. It wasn't a dog and never had been. It was only a big cardboard box. It was filled with dog collars. Some of those collars still had tags.

Dogs don't want revenge. That Akita didn't. I did. But how? The Akita? Or the Ladysmith? The dog or the gun? Either way, Reggie could take the fall for me. I talked to the dogs for a few minutes. Then I talked to Shane.

"This big guy here, the Akita?" I said. "He's called Romans Twelve Nineteen. Does that sound like a funny name for a dog? Romans Twelve Nineteen? It's a good name. It suits him. 'Vengeance is mine; I will repay, saith the Lord.' He will, too. The second I open this cage."

Rita claims to believe that what stayed my hand was some residual, hitherto unsuspected, reverence for human life. I have insisted, in her hearing, that if killing Shane could have restored the body of that black dog with the white splotch over his eye and on his tail, if it could have rebarked all the dogs Shane had debarked, if it could have undone everything he'd done, I wouldn't have hesitated, but my values are different from Rita's, and she doesn't like to realize how different. Rita is right about my reverence for life. All life. All lives. If I'd killed Shane, I'd have achieved more than revenge. I'd have saved the lives of all the dogs that would ever enter a laboratory of his again. What really stopped me was Rowdy. How sure was I that the Akita would go for Shane and not Rowdy? Rowdy wouldn't have run from the fight, and he wouldn't have stood a chance. He's my dog, and I love him, but I'm realistic about his limits. And how sure was I that Reggie would really end up taking the fall for everything? If not, where would Rowdy be? I also thought about Romans 12:19.

A tan phone hung on the wall above the counter, near the spot where Shane had been sitting when I'd walked in. I picked up the receiver and dialed Steve's number.

"This isn't about us," I said when I heard his voice. "It's about dogs. It's an emergency. Get every dog crate you own, load them in your van, and get over here. Fast. The door will be open. And bring a padlock." I gave him directions and hung up.

While I waited for Steve, I sat on the floor in front of Reggie's cage with the revolver aimed at him.

"Let me get this straight," I said. "Ed Nichols had you fill that prescription for the bee sting kit. You did. You ran all his errands. You ran that one. You went to

188

Quigley Drugs. It wasn't his usual drugstore. I'll bet that was Huron, but they might've remembered the prescription there. So you went to Quigley's, where the Nicholses would never have gone. Sissy waited on you, and she thought you were the one with the allergy. Right? Answer me fast, you bastard. Right?"

"Right." Reggie looked ridiculous and more than a little uncomfortable jammed in that cage, but no more than the dogs did in theirs.

"But you didn't know just how interested she was. You figured she'd never see you again, and even if she did, she wouldn't remember. But she did. First of all, she was a hypochondriac, and she was allergic to bees, or thought she was, and she practically wanted to start a support group for people who were. Second she always remembered what people filled prescriptions for because she liked to know people's secrets. Like Libby's. You know about that? You are not answering fast enough."

"Fits," he said.

"Seizures. That's the nice word for it. You could use an etiquette lesson. For example, when you answer me, you say, 'Yes, Miss Winter.' You can start now."

"Yes, Miss Winter."

"Very good. I get what happened at the show. You thought Sissy was going to say something about the prescription in front of Mimi. Then or later. And Mimi would have understood right away what it meant. Ed Nichols's old bee sting kit was at home? And Mimi found it there. She thought he hadn't taken it with him at all?"

He nodded his head.

"Now, tell me about Austin. That's still a little bit of a mystery to me. You got this crazy idea that I was

189

playing detective when all I was doing was trying to find a lost dog. You thought I was going to ask Austin something? What could I have asked him? Wait a minute. Let's back up. When you took that prescription to him instead of Huron, you had it planned, didn't you? I mean, why else would you go there? The people at Huron would've known the Nicholses. Quigley wouldn't. So you must've had it planned before you went on that fishing trip. Or maybe you just went prepared."

"It was an accident," he said.

"Don't give me that. You planned it all before you left Cambridge."

"No, listen. I'm carrying everything, and then we run into this buddy of mine, and he's half crocked, and he don't know nothing, and he don't keep his mouth shut. He starts in on the dogs."

"The pointers? They were with you? No. The dog scam. It went back that far? Before Shane was here? When Ed Nichols was still alive. And your buddy knew what you'd been up to in Cambridge. And he knew about Maine, too. Ed Nichols didn't know about that, did he? I bet I can guess. You used to break into camps, didn't you? When the people were away? What else?"

"Jacking deer. Everybody does it. It's no big deal."

"But Ed Nichols thought it was. And he trusted you. And then you ran into this guy who was so drunk he blurted out everything. And he did it in front of Ed Nichols, who must've been delighted to find out he'd hired a thief and that you were running a stolen-dog operation in his backyard."

Reggie stuck to the story, then and afterward, that he'd never planned to kill Ed Nichols. He also claimed, then and afterward, that he'd never stolen anything from the house or from Ed before Ed died, and he tried to deny that he'd stolen anything afterward, either. I didn't believe him, then or later. I've always suspected that Reggie's drunken friend said something Reggie never told me or anyone else, and that whatever it was confirmed something Ed Nichols had already begun to suspect. Or maybe it was what Ed Nichols saw. Maybe Reggie lifted a fly rod or a reel and sold it to the guy they ran into. Maybe the guy was carrying it, and Ed recognized it. I never found out for sure.

The outer door, the one to the corridor, swung open. Steve had never looked better, but I still hadn't forgiven him for Lady.

"Don't say anything," I said to him. "Go through that door. There's a black dog on the table. I'm almost sure he's dead, but I want you to check."

He was back almost immediately. "There's nothing I can do for him," Steve said. "He's gone."

"Okay. Let's get the ones in here out. Did you bring the padlock?"

He reached into the pocket of his battered denim jacket and pulled out the kind of combination padlock that's meant for bicycles.

"Give it to me," I said.

When I'd closed it on the latch of Reggie's cage, we started checking on the dogs and moving them out. It didn't take long. I got Rowdy and Clyde out first and put them both in the Bronco, with Rowdy in one of the crates Steve had brought and Clyde loose. Clyde hadn't made a sound. Then we got out as many dogs as Steve's van would hold, the golden who'd come when I called him, the shepherd-collie mix, the beagle, and the two brown dogs.

"The Akita?" I asked Steve.

191

"Do you want to open that cage?"

"No."

"You don't have something with you? A tranquilizer? There must be something here. Can't we shoot him up with something and carry him out? We can't just leave him."

"Holly, think about it. He was a beautiful dog once. It's too late."

"Damn! I'm calling Kevin," I said. "Then let's get out of here."

We split up in the parking lot. The drive back to my house took hardly any time at all. At the corner of Concord and Walden, Rowdy spotted a Bernese mountain dog pulling a small woman across the street. He growled and yelped. Clyde made not a sound. I hadn't found any shaved areas on his neck or any other signs of recent surgery. I'd started to ask Steve what it meant. Did it mean he was okay? Or could Shane have done the surgery without leaving a visible wound or scar? As I turned right onto Walden, I started to cry, and by the time I'd reached my house, I was sobbing and shaking.

CHAPTER 27

"THE VOICE OF HIM THAT CRIETH IN THE WILDERNESS," Mrs. Dennehy pronounced. "Prepare ye the way of the Lord, make straight in the desert a highway for our God."

With Mrs. Dennehy, in the beginning is always the Word. You eventually learn that quoting the Bible is sometimes nothing more than her way of saying hello. After that, the trick is to find one key word or phrase and ignore the others. Desert? A cold spring rain was pelting down on both of us and saturating Rowdy's absorbent double layers of soft undercoat and long guard hair. He'd hopped out of his crate in the back of the Bronco and down onto the driveway as cheerfully as if we'd been returning from a run around Fresh Pond. Voice that crieth? I'd stopped sobbing, and the light at the back of my house that illuminates the driveway wasn't bright enough to let her see my tears.

"He probably doesn't have a voice anymore," I said impatiently. "He can't cry out. I think he's been debarked. His vocal cords are gone. I've got to get him in the house and take a look at him, but Rowdy needs to go in first."

"And him going on and on this morning something awful, worrying the life out of Alicia. And how was she to know what he was going on about? Barking and howling to wake the dead, he was, she says to me, and neither of us thinking anything of it until Kevin comes home and tells me, poor thing, and Alicia calls and says she's afraid to be alone with a murderer running loose in the neighborhood. And her husband's gone out and him living next door to her all these years and mowing her lawn. Who would have thought it? First his mother, then his father."

"He didn't. Someone else did. And that dog is all right now. He's with some friends of mine. But I've got my father's dog here, and I'm not sure he's all right. And I'd like to get out of the rain." Mrs. Dennehy was wearing a raincoat. I wasn't.

"He maketh his sun to rise on the evil and on the good," she said, "and sendeth rain on the just and on the unjust."

Perhaps it was only her parting comment on the weather, but the words stayed with me as I led Rowdy into the house, shut him in my bedroom, pulled the ragged poncho over my damp clothes, grabbed a flashlight, then went back for Clyde, who'd meanwhile crawled into the crate.

"Hey, it's me," I told him. "Let's get you out of there."

When he didn't emerge from the crate, something told me not to put my hand in. The beam of the flashlight showed him curled up at the back of the crate, which wasn't a metal cage but one of the big airline-approved polypropylene crates with a metal mesh door at the front that had swung partly closed.

"Come on, Clyde. It's all over. It's all right now. I'm the one who got you out. Remember? Now let's go in the house so I can take a look at you. Come on. That's a good boy. You know me. Let's go."

At the sight of my hand on the crate door, he raised his upper lip in a silent display of a set of strong white teeth about twice the size of Rowdy's.

"Hey, what's the problem, big boy?"

He raised his lip again.

194

"Christ, growl at me," I said. "Please growl."

I started to pull the door slowly toward me. Clyde's eyes were huge with fear. The only sound he made was the snap of his jaws. I latched the door of the crate and left him locked in the Bronco.

"Buck? I've got Clyde," I said a few minutes later. "You were right. He was stolen."

After I gave him a brief account of the evening and an unrealistically optimistic report about Clyde, I did something I should have done earlier. I'd been feeling guilty about it all evening. I thanked him for the Ladysmith. And for once, I didn't remind him that Massachusetts has a tough handgun law. Reggie Cox and David Shane were probably both reminding the Cambridge police of the law already. According to state law, not only does the possession of a handgun without a permit carry a mandatory one-year jail term, but you can't even take your dog to jail with you. My only previous offenses consisted of the usual slew of unpaid parking tickets and two violations of the pooper-scooper law, but I knew the sentence was mandatory, and I assumed that fleeing to Maine wouldn't do me any good. It's not exactly Argentina. What had Rowdy done to deserve the punishment of having me locked up? The evil and the good, the just and the unjust. David Shane and Reggie Cox alive. Grover dead. Ed Nichols. Austin. Foolish Sissy. And poor Lady.

Even so, the last time I saw Steve Delaney, he was slamming the door of his van on a full load of rescued, crated dogs. He hadn't asked any questions. He'd shown up. He'd taken the dogs. Home, I assumed. And I'd never even offered to help with them. I'd never thanked him. Euthanasia wasn't his idea, I reminded myself. It was part of his job, a part he didn't like. But he did it, anyway. And I needed to know about debarking, about Clyde.

Why would anyone voluntarily live in an apartment over a veterinary clinic where he needs white-noise machines to drown out the sound of dogs? It wasn't just Cambridge rent. It was love of dogs. The lights were out above the clinic, but the ground-floor lights were on. I banged on the door.

He was wearing one of those loose green cotton tops he uses for surgery, the ones that bring out the color of his eyes. The rain had curled his hair without frizzing it. My mop of ringlets must have made me look like a cross between a golden retriever and a poodle.

"You look terrible," he said. "Come in."

His waiting room has the usual linoleum floor, high counter where the receptionist sits, benches for owners with neat stacks of *Dog's Life* and *Cat Fancy,* a big rack of pamphlets ("First Aid in Animal Emergencies," "Caring for the Aging Dog," "Housebreaking Your Puppy," "Urinary Tract Infections"), a poster depicting the life cycle of the heartworm, and two shelves with an array of sprays, powders, collars, and products to kill fleas and ticks. On one wall hang four framed, inexpert needlepoint pictures of terriers, a Scottie, a Yorkshire, an Airedale, and a Sealyham, all executed, no pun intended, by his mother. The room always smells of wet fur and Lysol with a hint of not-yet-disinfected urine, and blood, eye ointment, ear drops, cats with abscessed bites, aging setters, and puppies not quite house-trained, a sad, intense odor of life and death that frightens most dogs except Rowdy, who doesn't mind a hypodermic in the rear or up his nose if I hold him tightly and tell him what a good boy he is.

"Do you remember what I asked you after that
196

episode with your cousin Janice?" he said.

"I'll never do this again. I couldn't think of anyone else to call. And I thought maybe I was wrong. I thought maybe that big black dog might still be alive."

"For God's sake, Holly. How could he have been?"

"I know. It's just . . . I think I know whose dog he was. He belonged to a couple of kids, a family. I met the woman. Her name's Linda. I think I won't tell her. What's the point? Let her imagine him on a farm somewhere. She knows better, really, but she doesn't know, either. I didn't. Before."

He put an arm around my shoulders, but I didn't feel comforted. He took his arm away.

"You're in very big trouble, you know," he said.

"So were you. With me. I know, though. I understand. She didn't feel anything. She went to sleep. That's all she felt."

"Who?"

"Lady. The pointer bitch."

"I was talking about the gun," he said.

"Yeah. I've been thinking about it, but there's nothing I can do. It's a little late to go and apply for a permit. I practically forgot the thing was there. In my closet. I was going to take it to Maine the next time I went home. I didn't exactly want to toss it in the trash. And then, there it was. And what would I have done without it? I'd be dead. All the time I was trying to find Clyde, Reggie Cox misinterpreted everything I did, you know, everything I said. He actually thought I was investigating him or something."

"He thought you were playing Nancy Drew?"

"And I never even read Nancy Drew," I said. "I read Jack London and Albert Payson Terhune. So show me the dogs, and we'll figure out what to do with them.

197

That's what I came for."

"Is that all?"

"More or less."

"Mostly less."

"Yeah. Look, I understand. I don't hold it against you. It's just me. I can't . . . And I'll never call you again for anything like tonight. I mean, why would I? I'll probably never see the inside of a lab again. I know how much trouble it could mean for you. I'm sorry."

"It's okay," he said. "I'm sorry about the black dog. And the Akita."

"But not about Lady," I said.

"No." He smiled. I hated him for that. "Let's take a look at the dogs."

I followed him through the door to the back area that's filled with cabinets of veterinary supplies and medicine, then through another door. The dogs were a little more crowded than I'd have liked to see them, but less than they had been a few hours earlier, and, although as silent as before, they were safe. The two brown dogs were sharing a single cage. In his cage, the beagle hadn't given up trying to bay and yelp. The golden was wagging his tail. All of the cages were full. One occupant had been evicted to make room for the newcomers. She ran up to me when we walked in. She wasn't the pointer Max was, of course. She lacked his self-confidence, and although she wasn't a runty little pet shop specimen like Zip, she was small and quivery and as love hungry as when I'd met her in Sissy Quigley's backyard.

"I can't always do this," Steve said. "You have to get that. I can't. I can't even keep her upstairs with India yet. I'm working on it. But you have to know. There are limits. I can't save them all."

198

CHAPTER 28

"I'D HAVE TO ANESTHETIZE HIM," STEVE SAID. "I'D have to open his mouth wide. You need to see the larynx. He won't let me look. Most dogs won't."

We were standing in my driveway with the tailgate of the Bronco open. In the early morning light, we got a better view inside Clyde's crate than I'd had the night before, but he looked just as terror-stricken as he had then.

"There's no scar at all? It doesn't show?"

"It's usually done through the mouth. There's another way, but it involves major surgery. You make an incision under the neck, and you approach the larynx that way. I've only read about it. They wouldn't do that in a research lab. They'd go through the mouth."

"So what do we do?"

"Keep an eye on him. The main thing is to watch for complications."

"Like what?"

"Well, what happens when a dog barks is that the vocal folds vibrate, and what you do is go in and cut out that tissue. So one risk is that when scar tissue forms, it can begin to close the glottis. And the vocal folds protect the trachea, so once they're gone, the dog can aspirate into the trachea. I won't do it."

"Of course not."

He shrugged. "A lot of people, especially old-timers, do it all the time. People want it sometimes. They live in small apartments, and the landlords are going to evict them if the dog makes noise. If it's the only way to keep the dog . . ."

"It's grotesque."

"There's too much risk. Especially aspiration."

"I hate the whole idea."

"Sometimes the scar tissue re-forms a sort of fold."

"And the bark comes back?"

He nodded. "A hoarse bark."

"Not that howl, though. How am I going to tell my father?"

"Don't," he said gently. "We don't know for sure. Don't tell him unless you have to."

At eleven, after Steve left, Kevin showed up at my back door. As I've said, I'd suspected him of having a crush on me, although I couldn't see any sign of it then. He was red in the face and cold in the voice.

"Don't touch a thing in Shane's apartment," he said. "And don't make any plans for this afternoon. You will be deposed at three o'clock."

"And I was just getting used to the throne," I said. If puns are bad enough, they usually win him over, but that one failed.

"Be there."

He handed me a plain white envelope and loped off toward Fresh Pond, where he trains for the Boston Marathon. I admire him. If it weren't for dogs, my running muscles would have atrophied within a couple of years of my birth. I might never even have bothered learning to walk at all.

Before I had a chance to open the envelope, my father's van pulled in. Clyde was still denned up at the back of the crate, and I still didn't know whether he had a voice left. The front windows of the Bronco were both open a crack, and I'd eased open the tailgate and sneaked a bowl of water and one of Eukanuba laced with grated Cheddar into the back near the crate, but I couldn't see any sign that Clyde had touched them.

200

"What kind of shape's he in?" my father greeted me.

If Rowdy had been outside, Buck might have said hello to him.

"He won't come out of the crate. I got a pretty good look at him, and I think he's mostly okay. Physically. But he crawled into the crate, and he won't come out. In the back of my car. As soon as I get near him, he snaps at me. And he means business."

Buck nodded.

"I got some food and water in," I continued, "but I don't think he's touched them. I even tried a doughnut, and that didn't work. I didn't want to try anything else. He's scared almost to death, I think. I'm sure he'd have bitten me."

At two-thirty, when I left for the police station in his van, Buck was still patiently sitting in the driver's seat of the Bronco. He'd read the *Sunday Globe*, including an account of the previous evening's events, six or eight back issues of *Dog's Life*, and a year's worth of *New England Obedience News* and *Northeast Canine Companion*. In between, he'd been singing. "Clementine." "America the Beautiful." And, yes, the torment of my childhood, "Deck the Halls with Boughs of Holly."

After dark, when I returned, he was still there.

"From the halls of Montezuma to the shores of Tripoli," he was singing.

"How's it going?" I asked softly.

"Fine. At the end of the Marines' Hymn, I make my move. Out of the front seat."

"Is the crate shut?"

It wasn't.

I checked on them about every half hour throughout the evening. Buck's voice sounded increasingly hoarse, but at ten, he was stretched out on the floor next to the crate.

"I don't suppose you'd consider putting your feet instead of your face next to the door of the crate," I said. "Prosthetic feet are easier to come by than a prosthetic head."

"Ye of little faith," he whispered.

If Clyde had howled, I'd have heard him. I didn't ask whether he'd whined or yipped. Sometime in the night, Buck came into the house, used the bathroom, and made noise in the kitchen. At five in the morning, I found him asleep in the back of the Bronco. Clyde was still in the crate, but his nose was sticking out. By seven, Buck had one hand in front of Clyde's nose, not one inch from those teeth.

"It's like taming a wild animal," I said to Steve when he called.

"You want me to bring something over?" he offered. "A mild sedative? It won't do him any harm. Anything they gave him is out of his system by now."

"Buck needs to do this himself. Thanks."

It took him the rest of the day. At dusk, they both climbed out of the Bronco, and Buck led Clyde slowly toward the van. Just then, a cruiser tore down Concord Avenue, siren wailing. Clyde lifted his great head to the sky and answered its wail with that same howl that had always given me shivers. My father was too busy watching Clyde to notice my face. They got into the van and drove off.

Why was Clyde spared? I think maybe because he was silent already, too terrified to make a sound. Buck would probably know, but I've never told him what almost happened to Clyde. What did happen was hard enough for Buck. Clyde, who used to go everywhere

202

with my father, hasn't left Owls Head since then. Buck won't admit it, but Clyde has never been the same since. Buck doesn't trust him anymore, not around other people.

That evening, during a hard rain, after we made sure Kevin wasn't home, Rita and I took my master key and let ourselves into the third-floor apartment. David Shane was still in the hospital.

"What's he still there for?" Rita asked. "You didn't shoot him. Or did you?"

"I didn't," I said. "I should have."

"So why's he there? What's the problem?"

"Submissive urination," I said.

Windy had spotted all over everything, but since Rita had been feeding her and taking her out now and then, she was fine. With Windy temporarily locked in the bathroom, the two of us shoved, hauled, tugged, and dragged the white leather couch down the back stairs, out the door, and onto the sidewalk, where some lucky trash-picker would snatch it up before morning.

"This is acting out," Rita said as we stood in my kitchen drying our sopping hair on dish towels. "It's going to cost me an extra year of analysis."

"So don't tell your analyst."

"I have to."

"You don't have to do anything. Besides, there's nothing wrong with it. It's just a creative eviction notice. I'm the landlord. I'm entitled."

"I'm not."

"You didn't see that place, Rita. If you had, you'd realize there's nothing to feel guilty about. And could you honestly live here with him on the third floor? Are you going to move? I have to get rid of him. Honest to God, Rita, I was such a fool. Everybody else knew what a vapid louse he was. Kevin. Matt Gerson. My father. Everybody but me. You know what I've been wondering?"

"What the hell you were doing exposing yourself to such risk."

"No."

"What it meant that you took that gun, a gift from your father. No? If this is about dogs, I don't want to hear it."

"You're a therapist. You have to listen."

"I'm not your therapist. I'm your tenant."

"You're my friend."

"Spit it out."

"Look, Rita, I've been examining my conscience, and here's what I've seen. Every dog I've ever had has been beautiful. I have not owned one ugly dog or even one ordinary dog. I've probably owned the most beautiful dogs in the world. And what I've been thinking is that it's so superficial. I treat them like decorations. And that's more or less how I reacted to Shane. I liked looking at him. He flattered me. He got me to talk. I didn't really take in anything about him. For example, if I hadn't been such a fool, I'd have noticed something about the couch and also the Mercedes. It has real leather upholstery, you know. The man wasn't happy unless he was sitting on dead animals. That should've told me something. So what does all of it say about me? Look, suppose Rowdy suddenly turned into an ordinary dog. Or what if Vinnie had? Now, she was a really beautiful bitch. You remember her."

"Holly? Look, sometimes reality is the best medicine. I hate to be the one to tell you this, but Vinnie looked exactly like every other golden retriever."

"She did not!"

"And you know what else? Rowdy looks like a thousand other malamutes. He can't turn ordinary-looking. He already is."

"How can you say that! Look at him!"

He was asleep on the kitchen floor, stretched out to his full, glorious length, his body strong and compact, his coat thick, dense, coarse, and not too long, his head broad, his ears flawless wedges, his muzzle neither long and pointed nor stubby, his legs heavily boned and muscled, in other words, exactly the way the standard of the breed says an Alaskan malamute is supposed to be. The standard is an ideal, an abstract portrait of the perfect dog. My perfect dog.

"How would you like me to say that Groucho is ordinary?" I added.

"He *is* ordinary. Except to me. You saw this jerk, Shane, and you got seduced by his good looks. So he told you your hair was pretty or something. He didn't tell you to quit talking about dogs. He didn't say he was sick of hearing about your father. Big deal. So it's superficial. It's ordinary. We're all ordinary. Welcome to the human race."

CHAPTER 29

SOME OF US ARE LESS ORDINARY THAN OTHERS. TAKE the rich. Scott Fitzgerald was right. The very rich really are different from you and me. They are extraordinarily naive. It's a luxury they can afford. Take Mimi. Nothing I could say would persuade her that my sole object, right from the beginning, had been to recover a lost dog.

We sat in one of the rooms I'd been in at the fundraiser, a magnified living room with four couches, each with matching upholstered chairs and a polished coffee table. Pretty wooden chairs. Side tables. Standing lamps. Are knickknacks in bad taste? There weren't any unless you count the candlesticks with long tapers on the mantles above the fireplaces and, on the tables, those extravagantly perishable knickknacks, baskets of out-of-season flowers, blue delphiniums, yellow lilies, white baby's breath with their stems embedded in Oasis masked by swathes of sphagnum moss.

I'd just taken a seat on one of the couches when Zip ran in and urinated on the rug.

"Damn," Mimi said. "The problem is, she likes you. It happens when she's overexuberant."

Positive reframing, Rita calls it. If a guy spits on you, he washed your face.

"It's your rug."

Mimi made no move at all to clean up after Zip. Someone else would do it. Her tail between her legs, Zip quivered and shook, pawed at me, then fell onto the floor in a shivering, neurotic mass that should never have been bred. Go right ahead. Buy from a pet shop.

"I feel as though I owe you some explanation," Mimi

said.

"Not really." I smiled.

She was sitting in an upholstered wing-back chair that matched the blue flowered pattern of the couch. If I'd been invited to drop in for lunch with Mrs. Bush, Millie, and the pups, I'd have tried to buy a duplicate of the suit she wore, but I probably wouldn't have been able to pay for it. It was dark green, and under the jacket was a cowl-necked white sweater knitted from some blend of exotic fibers. I wanted to ask her where she donated her clothes after she wore them once.

"He had me completely fooled, you know," she said. "I was totally taken in."

"I never thought you knew. I mean, I'm sure you had no idea at all what he was up to. No one thinks that."

"I'd like to tell you about it, if you don't mind. It's on my conscience, so to speak."

"If you want," I said. "You know, I don't hold it against you."

"I appreciate that." She leaned back in the chair and folded her hands in her lap, ever Ron's perfect lady. "I appreciate everything you've done."

I shrugged. "I had to get my father's dog back. Everything else was an accident, sort of. It wasn't anything more than sort of a combination of bad luck and good luck."

She smiled one of those almost expressionless smiles and patted the air with one hand, gesturing me to put a lid on what she misinterpreted as false modesty, I guess.

"This has been a very difficult time for me." Her articulation was, as always, clean, and her voice strong. "Among other things, I have set myself the task of doing what I can to make reparations for my part in this, however unintended it was. I harbored a criminal."

207

"Look, you supported the ordinance long before you had a clue about what was going on with him. You've done more to promote that than anybody else. If you're feeling guilty, think about that. The rest of us are the ones who should feel guilty for not doing everything we could."

"Thank you. But I've had to realize that I exercised extremely poor judgment, to say the least, and with terrible consequences."

"Come on! He took advantage of you."

"That's true. But that's not all of it. And, of course, I do recognize that I wasn't alone in showing poor judgment. Some of it was Ed's responsibility, too. In effect, we let the man make fools of both of us." Her hands were folded on her lap again. She looked perfectly composed.

"I think you're blaming yourself too much," I said. "Practically everyone else was taken in, too." As I'd been by David Shane.

"That's just it!" she said, sitting forward and making a fist with one hand. "And he really was so wonderfully capable. He seemed completely reliable. And I see now that Ed and I both romanticized him. We thought he was a child of nature, I suppose. He seemed unspoiled." She sounded momentarily bitter. "And he was unbelievably useful! He literally could do anything."

"And would."

"Yes." She paused. "I see what you mean. One doesn't imagine the existence of people like that, people without limits. One assumes that the boundaries are there, as they are for oneself. We all did. Libby certainly did, too. He could be very, very seductive."

"Your husband never had any questions about him? He never wondered about anything?"

Zip got up and shook her way over to me. I rubbed her silly head.

"Oh, he had a few . . . Well, they were nothing more than minor gripes, really. Ed would complain that he'd use my car too often." Her car, the green station wagon with the barrier in the back. "And when we first had him here, Ed had to speak to him a couple of times about cleaning himself up. Taking a shower. That sort of thing. But I'm sure he did it tactfully. So, no. So far as I know, Ed trusted him completely. We both did."

"And when your husband died, you had no suspicions at all?"

"Why would I? I found the kit myself, right here in this house. I knew what it was. You know what a kit is?"

"Epinephrine."

Zip was staring up pathetically at Mimi and raking her skirt with a forepaw.

"With a syringe," Mimi said. "And Ed always made light of the problem. He pooh-poohed it. You know, that's one of the reasons I never dreamed . . . Because here we're only a block away from the Mt. Auburn emergency room, and he didn't like the idea of the kit because if it's not used just so, it can cause gangrene. Zip, do stop it."

"So you thought that was why he left the kit here?"

"Oh, he didn't leave it deliberately, no. Logically, he understood. But, afterward, I thought that, unconsciously, it must have been that fear, in combination with how he hated to be fussed over. He didn't want to be treated like an invalid. That was another thing, of course. Like every other man, he hated the idea of looking weak. So, afterward, I thought, well, of course, there he was, participating in this male rite,

209

roughing it in the north woods and so forth. He loved that. He lived for those fishing and hunting trips. And naturally, he didn't want to seem like some big baby."

"It must have made sense."

"Believe me, it did. And, of course, Reggie Cox was right there! And it never occurred to me to doubt a single thing he said. So I thought I knew exactly what had happened. He told me all about it, of course. And I was devastated. But Reggie seemed like a godsend. Afterward, I was afraid to stay in the house alone, without a man, and there he was, when he drove the car home. Also I felt responsible. I thought he must be afraid that it meant losing his job. So he stayed."

"And at the show?"

"I can only say that I must have taken his presence for granted. Lately, of course, if he wasn't right there, he was with Libby, and I never minded. On the contrary, I was happy to see them both find a relationship. I thought they were good for each other." She sighed. "And, in a way, I thought it was cute, somehow. That's why he was at the show, of course, because of Libby. As their romance unfolded, he began to spend more and more time with her. It wasn't part of his job to be there."

"So that's why he hadn't run into Sissy before."

She nodded. "He knew nothing about showing dogs. He knew nothing about handling. He had no interest, really. But, of course, he seemed to have that wonderful way with dogs."

"He did. Rowdy loved him. That's my dog, Rowdy."

"Of course. Now, he's an Alaskan malamute? Not a Siberian husky."

I smiled. "That's right."

"Just this morning, I reserved a pointer puppy. It seems like a way to start recovering, for Libby as well as for me. We hope we'll have a mate for Sunshine, but Libby says we aren't to count on it."

"Libby knows a lot about dogs."

"Doesn't she! This puppy will be good for both of us, after what we've been through. Libby especially needs something. She met him here, of course, and through me."

When I got home, my answering machine had a message from Libby Knowles. I returned the call.

"Holly? Look, I know this may sound coldhearted, but you understand about dogs, and you can ask better than I can. Could you find out if I can have my shears back now?"

"Libby, tell me something. Why did you ever buy those gigantic shears in the first place? I've never seen you with a giant dog."

"You don't know much about grooming, do you?" It wasn't a question.

"No, I don't know much about it at all."

"Well, you don't fit the shears to the dog. If you're a professional, you've got control of shears like that, and you use them whenever you want to scissor, on any scissorable dog."

"You don't scissor pointers. Or goldens."

"I don't handle all the dogs I groom. I do Old English sheepdogs. I've done Portuguese water spaniels. You know something else? The blades are probably dull now. And it costs thirty dollars to sharpen them."

"Libby doesn't care where they've been," I told Kevin. "She doesn't care who put them there. It bothers her that they might be dull. She doesn't care at all how they got that way. And what about Mimi? I wonder if this whole thing has wised her up at all."

211

He was standing at my kitchen stove burning onions.

"You're hard on Mrs. Nichols," he said.

"I like her."

"You're still hard on her."

"She's so trusting, Kevin. She thinks everyone is the way *she* is. Genuine. That's what I like about her. She's genuine. And she does a lot of good."

"You bet she does. Look at that poor slob, Pete Quigley. You want some?"

He spooned the greasy mess onto a burned hamburger. I didn't have the guts to tell him that I hadn't been able to eat meat since I'd seen the inner room of that lab.

"No thanks," I said. "I just ate. It was nice of Mimi to offer to buy the drugstore. It was a lot kinder than just giving Pete money outright, you know, as if he were some charity case or as if she were paying for his parents, and the money undid everything and made it all right. And it's not as if she had any use for it. What's she going to do with a run-down drugstore?"

"Tear it down. Leave it. It doesn't matter to her, does it?"

"Speaking of the drugstore, did you ever find out about Reggie going there? He was after whatever record there was of that prescription, right?"

"Right."

"But why did he wait? Once he'd decided I was onto him, and if he wanted to destroy the records, why did he wait?"

"Your friend. The girlfriend who wants the shears back. Apparently she and Cox had a little game going whereby whenever Mrs. Nichols takes off somewhere, and she gives the help time off, they move in."

"Into the main part of the house?"

212

"Yeah. Live it up. You know. Get out the fancy glasses. Take a bath in her tub. Sleep in her bed."

"They probably didn't even change the sheets."

Kevin laughed.

"Mimi Nichols doesn't know about this, does she?" I asked. "She couldn't."

"I didn't tell her."

"You can bet Libby didn't, either," I said.

"So that's where he was. On a heavy date."

"You want some blueberry pie?" I asked. "Don't worry. I didn't make it. But it's made with real Maine blueberries. They probably came from Deblois. It's good."

"Sure. How come you can't cook?"

"If I could, you'd marry me. So would Steve. And there I'd be, a bigamist. And if I knew how to cook, I'd get stuck doing it, and it's a waste of time."

"Unlike dogs," Kevin said.

"Bigamy reminds me of my other little crime."

"Little."

"Yeah," I said. "A year in jail isn't little. I know. Look, I know you took a big risk doing that."

He'd eaten the last of his pie and was scraping the plate with his fork.

"Are you listening?" I added. "I'd never have asked you to do it, you know. It never crossed my mind. Even if it had, I wouldn't have asked you."

"Just do me a favor." His expression was serious. "Two favors."

"Sure. Of course."

"One, don't say anything about it. Not a thing."

"Of course not. I know better than that."

"Two. Get rid of the damned thing."

"Kevin, that's foolish. Why should I? I mean, I do have a permit for it."

CHAPTER 30

A COUPLE OF WEEKS LATER, THE LETTER CARRIER LEFT me a big brown Jiffy mailing envelope with no return address. Inside were photocopies of research protocols from a place called Massachusetts Primate Institute, which was and still is located in one of the almost-rural suburbs beyond Route 128. I read the protocols. They were obscene. Dogs aren't even primates, for God's sake. They're carnivores. Or they used to be. The researchers at the Massachusetts Primate Institute had apparently expanded the order of primates to include any animal that objects to surgery without anesthesia. People are already primates, of course. Watch out. You might be next.

I remembered something Matt Gerson had said to me when it was all over. "Who do you think these people are, Holly?" he'd said. "These researchers. You think they look like monsters? They go around with dog blood dripping off their hands? You think they talk about it? Some of them do. They say they do research. Some of them don't. The only dogs they talk about are the ones they keep at home, the family dogs. But they all look just like everyone else."

Two nights after the big envelope was delivered, the phone rang.

"Don't hang up." The voice sounded older than I remembered, more a man's than a boy's now.

"I didn't intend to."

"I read about what you did. Don't hang up."

"Am I hanging up?"

"I have a job at Mass. Primate. Temporary. Are you listening?"

"Yes."

"This job ends tonight. Sometime around eleven. Have you got a van?"

"A Bronco. A big one."

"Gas it up. Leave your dogs home."

"I only have one."

"I'll have the crates. All you're going to do is drive. You won't be inside." He gave me directions. "Holly?"

"I'm here."

"Don't let me down."

I started to say that I don't condone violence. Then I thought about it. "I'm on your side," I said. "I always have been."

One Sunday in early June, Steve and I took the dogs— Rowdy, India, Lady—for a walk in the woods in a park in Newton that's only twenty minutes from Cambridge. It isn't exactly the woods, but it reminds me of real woods when I start to get homesick.

"You're not that different from Mimi Nichols," Steve said. "There are some realities you just don't see. Or won't."

"How can you say that? You saw that lab. You saw what I saw. If that isn't reality, what is?"

"That it was legal," he said. "That it *is* legal."

"That's not my reality. That's not my law. It isn't yours, either."

"How many laws do you think there are?"

"If either of us made the law," I said, "that son of a bitch would be locked up and never get out. You know that."

"That's what I mean," he said. "The reality is that we don't control it. We just do what we can. That's all."

"It isn't much," I said. Lately, what I'd been able to

215

do had begun to include a few activities he didn't know about. It seems inevitable that he'll eventually begin to suspect, but he hasn't yet. And I won't drag him in. I promised not to do that again.

"He didn't do anything illegal," Steve said. "Look, I know. I hate it, too. They aren't even going to get him for buying stolen property, dogs or anything else."

"He has a good lawyer. All he had to do was claim he didn't know. I wish Reggie Cox had had the sense to steal one of the Matisses. Shane couldn't have claimed he didn't know what it was."

"They'll get Reggie Cox, though," Steve said. "Isn't that some consolation?"

"Sort of. Yes, of course. But you know what? They probably won't even bother prosecuting him for stealing the dogs. And you know what punishment Shane gets for buying them and torturing them? He gets evicted from his apartment."

"He could've fought that. It wasn't a legal eviction."

"Oh, yes, it was." I was adamant.

"It was not. You know that. And he got denied tenure."

"Big deal. He'll go somewhere else now."

"Sure he will," Steve said. "He's a bastard. But he's not a criminal, not in the eyes of the law."

He was in my book.

EPILOGUE

ON MONDAY, JUNE 26, 1989, THE CAMBRIDGE CITY Council passed the ordinance that made Cambridge, Massachusetts, the first city in the United States to regulate animal research. Steve was in the council chambers when the ordinance was passed. So was Mimi Nichols, he told me. So were a lot of other animal rights advocates. Everyone applauded and cheered. It's a wishy-washy ordinance, but it's better than nothing. That's what other cities have: nothing. I'd like to have been there when the city council passed that ordinance, but I had to be elsewhere that evening. I'd passed my own ordinance. There was someplace I had to be. There was something I had to do.

Dear Reader:

I hope you enjoyed reading this Large Print mystery. If you are interested in reading other Beeler Large Print Mystery titles or any other Beeler Large Print titles, ask your librarian or write to me at:

Thomas T. Beeler, *Publisher*
Post Office Box 659
Hampton Falls, New Hampshire 03844

You can also call me at 1-800-818-7574 and I will send you my latest catalogue.

Audrey Lesko chooses the titles I publish in Large Print. Our aim is to provide good books by outstanding authors—books we both enjoyed reading and liked well enough to want to share. We warmly welcome any suggestions for new titles and authors.

Sincerely,